### "What the hell is wrong with me?"

Ice smoothed his hand over his short, coarse hair, twisting his neck from side to side. In this predawn hour, his favorite time for writing, he had the main room of the hotel suite to himself. He should be writing full blast right now, but he couldn't get a handle on the script for this pilot.

The problem was Andrea Lovette. She kept invading his thoughts. He'd tossed and turned all night, his dreams one sexual adventure after another with her in the lead role. Damn. It was nuts. She wasn't even his type. Too curvy, too in-his-face, too kiss-my-ass. *Too much like me. It takes one to know one.*

But that wasn't all. Whenever their eyes met, he felt a shift in his equilibrium, as though the ground had cracked open beneath his feet, leaving him with a sense of standing on two halves of a chasm. If he weren't careful, he might fall into the abyss. He grinned, recalling her reaction to his offer of sex. Damn, he couldn't deny he'd wanted her then, and that if they'd been alone, he might have acted on that baser instinct.

The idea had him smiling harder...

# Acclaim for the Big Sky Pie Series

## Delightful

"I expected to enjoy it like I do so many other romances, finish it, sigh happily, and then go to sleep. I didn't expect to cry or get butterflies in my stomach...or get that full, tense, heart-pounding feeling in my gut that you get when you're falling in love. Yeah I felt that. Adrianne Lee did such a good job writing the falling-in-love part that I felt it too."

—RandomBookMuses.com

"Fabulous...a fun and sexy romance. Lee keeps the series fresh with unique storylines and unpredictable pairings."          —BookReviewsandMorebyKathy.com

## Delicious

"*Delicious* deserves four big, yummy, juicy stars...Lee gives her readers mesmerizing descriptions of baking pies, wonderful characters, and a fresh take on love."

—RandomBookMuses.com

"Five Big Sky blueberry pies for this fabulous romantic page-turner...You'll want to savor each slice of this scrumptious series."          —TheBestReviews.com

"Fast-paced and engaging...a wonderful addition to Lee's heartwarming series."

—BookReviewsandMorebyKathy.com

## Delectable

"For a fun, light, and entertaining read about second chances, don't miss *Delectable*."

—HarlequinJunkie.com

"I found *Delectable* so refreshing!...True love and homemade pies made this totally delectable!"

—RandomBookMuses.com

"A nice second-chance love story with good main and secondary characters. I enjoyed the read and am looking forward to the second book in this series."

—SexyBookTimes.com

"A positively charming romance that is incredibly heartwarming...a fast-paced and engaging novel that is sure to delight anyone who enjoys homespun love stories." —BookReviewsandMorebyKathy.com

*Delightful*

# Also by Adrianne Lee

*Delectable*
*Delicious*
*Decadent*

# Delightful

Adrianne Lee

**FOREVER**

NEW YORK   BOSTON

Copyright © 2014 by Adrianne Lee
Excerpt from *Delectable* copyright © 2013 by Adrianne Lee
All rights reserved. In accordance with the U.S. Copyright Act of 1976, the scanning, uploading, and electronic sharing of any part of this book without the permission of the publisher is unlawful piracy and theft of the author's intellectual property. If you would like to use material from the book (other than for review purposes), prior written permission must be obtained by contacting the publisher at permissions@hbgusa.com. Thank you for your support of the author's rights.

Forever
Hachette Book Group
1290 Avenue of the Americas
New York, NY 10104

www.HachetteBookGroup.com

Originally published as an ebook

First mass market edition: November 2014
10 9 8 7 6 5 4 3 2 1

OPM

Forever is an imprint of Grand Central Publishing.
The Forever name and logo are trademarks of Hachette Book Group, Inc.

The publisher is not responsible for websites (or their content) that are not owned by the publisher.

The Hachette Speakers Bureau provides a wide range of authors for speaking events. To find out more, go to www.hachettespeakersbureau.com or call (866) 376-6591.

**ATTENTION CORPORATIONS AND ORGANIZATIONS:**
Most Hachette Book Group books are available at quantity discounts with bulk purchase for educational, business, or sales promotional use. For information, please call or write:

**Special Markets Department, Hachette Book Group**
**1290 Avenue of the Americas, New York, NY 10104**
**Telephone: 1-800-222-6747  Fax: 1-800-477-5925**

*For Jami Davenport, a plotting genius, my personal cheerleader who writes really great male POV.*

# Acknowledgments

Thank You:

Larry and Spooky—for making me laugh when I most need it.

Kate Cassidy, registered sanitarian with Flathead City-County Health Department—for helping me keep the facts straight.

Karen Papandrew—for having an eagle editing eye, and for offers of help and cheering me on when I needed both.

Gail Fortune—my fabulous agent.

Jessica Bromberg—for offering me so many promotional opportunities.

Claire Brown—for giving the Big Sky Pie series such great covers.

Alex Logan—for her red pen edits, her knowledge of punctuation, her hard work on my behalf, and all the times she makes me smile.

*Delightful*

# Chapter One

"A couple of bites of my caramel apple pie and a man will look puppy-eyed at you," Molly McCoy, proprietor of Big Sky Pie, said. "A whole slice and he's liable to get down on one knee and offer a ring."

"Hah," Andrea Lovette, assistant manager of the Kalispell, Montana, pie shop, scoffed as she filled in the space for *Specialty of the Month* on the blackboard menu. "Oh, I'll give you that the pie smells like a little piece of heaven, but if all it took to snag a husband was a delightful mix of cinnamon, caramel, and green apple stuffed into a flaky, buttery crust, every marriage-minded female this side of Flat Head Lake would be flocking to our doorstep in droves. And that is sadly not the case."

"I'm worried about the falling receipts, too, dear."

Only Molly—red hair spiked, bright blue eyes full of smiles, wiping her hands on her apron as she surveyed the café and nodding approval—didn't look worried. Sunlight spilled into the room, glancing off the red tablecloths, beige walls, and accents of white. The space had the warm ambience of a tearoom. "It's a known fact that restaurants generally lose money the first year or two after opening. I discussed that with my accountant before I applied for a building permit to remodel this place. So stop fretting."

"But we started out with such a bang." Andrea leaned back slightly on the stepladder and studied her handiwork, checking the lettering for spelling and readability. Satisfied, she descended the ladder, set it behind the front counter, and glanced around the empty café, each booth and table set and ready for customers. If only some would come in. She met Molly's gaze. "That huge chamber of commerce event at the mall, our grand opening gala, catering a couple of weddings and anniversary parties..."

Molly helped herself to tea. "Summer is always going to be a big season for us with all the tourists adding to the regular customers, but we have to expect business will dip once autumn arrives. Folks are busy gearing up for winter, or dieting before the holidays, or school's starting."

Seeking a diversion, Andrea glanced out the front windows. No cars in the parking lot, no one walking toward the door. She sighed. "I guess being a single mom of two, I'm always thinking of the budget's bottom line."

"You need something else to busy your mind. Like a man."

"Okay, there seems to be a theme to this conversation." *A theme about me, men, and marriage.* Andrea strode to the coffee counter, refilled her mug, and added a layer of caffeine to the anxiety in her stomach. "You aren't adding matchmaker to your résumé, are you?"

"No, dear." Molly retied her apron around her middle, a middle that had shrunk considerably since her triple-bypass surgery four months ago. The heart-healthy diet was doing wonders for her figure, even if she grumbled constantly about "rabbit fodder." But now there was a mother-knows-all expression in her twinkly blue eyes. "I just noticed that wistful look you had at Nick and Jane's wedding this past summer. The same look that comes over you whenever Quint and Callee are in here together. You miss having a steady fella in your life."

Andrea breathed a little easier, tucking a strand of thick blond hair behind one ear, glad that there were no blind-date setups to cancel. On some level, she knew what Molly said was true, but she found herself denying it. "No. I don't."

"You do." Molly gave her a sad, indulgent smile. "Maybe it just takes one to know one, dear."

Andrea's heart clutched. Molly had lost her husband suddenly last winter, and his loss was still keen. She crossed to Molly and hugged her around the shoulders. "Donnie Lovette was no Jimmy McCoy. He was not the love of my life. I was young and stupid and should never have eloped with him or agreed to spend our first years on the rodeo circuit. My sons paid for those bad decisions." *Were still paying.*

"Ah, but then you wouldn't have had Logan and Lucas, and your life would be so much poorer for it."

Andrea couldn't dispute that. Her sons were the only two things she and Donnie had gotten right. "But if I had it to do over, I'd only consider marrying someone who would make a great father, someone steady that the boys and I could count on."

"You'd marry someone you didn't love?"

She shrugged. "If he was a great father, sure. Why not? Love is overrated."

Molly's eyebrows rose in disbelief. "You've seen proof to the contrary of that lately, right here in this very pie shop."

Andrea moaned to herself. "Yeah, well, I'm too busy for a serious relationship."

Molly laughed. "Love doesn't work like that. It's inconvenient. Messy. It comes along when you least expect it, or aren't looking for it, or really can't see how to fit it into your life."

*That's a scary notion.* Was it true? Andrea wouldn't know. What she thought was love when she married Donnie had more likely been raging teenage hormones. She'd never met a guy who'd made her feel whatever it was she saw in Callee's and Jane's eyes. She probably never would, given her weakness.

When it came to the opposite sex, her radar zeroed in on bad boys as if it were hardwired into her genes. She couldn't help herself. Line up a wall of eligible husband-types, toss in a confirmed bachelor, blind-fold her, and she would chose the one-night-stand guy. Every. Single. Time. It was her fatal flaw, the thing she would change about herself, if she could. That thing she could never tell Molly.

"You know, this is just the kind of conversation that would be great on our reality show," Molly said, sipping her tea with the innocence of the Pope.

Andrea winced. This past summer, without bothering to first okay it with her staff, Molly had contracted with a Los Angeles production team for a pilot to be shot and shopped to the networks. Filming was supposed to commence by the end of this week. Even though the staff voted to go forward with the pilot, the closer the time came for shooting to start, the more misgivings Andrea had.

And the giddier Molly became. "I can't wait for the camera crew to show up."

Andrea could wait. She foresaw nothing but chaos and disaster in this undertaking. There was too much potential for things to go wrong. Close-the-shop wrong. "I have some serious reservations about the reality show. This is a small town. The bulk of our customers are people we know."

"Don't you see? That's the beauty of it. They'll tell their friends and family to watch the show. It will up our viewers and our ratings."

Andrea wondered why Molly couldn't see the pit-falls. The downside. "We'll become instant celebrities. The public will feel as if they know us personally. We'll have no buffer between them and us. Anything we say on the show is going to be out there, reviewed, dissected, analyzed. Everyone will be gossiping about us."

Molly's grin widened. "Of course they will. And they'll be coming in for pie."

"But have you seen how cutthroat shows like *Project Runway* and *Survivor* can be?"

Molly shook her head, giving a dismissive wave of her hand. "Those shows are contests. We're a family here. We'll be more like...the Kardashians."

Every bad consequence Andrea had ever imagined bounced through her mind.

"Besides, dear," Molly said, "we need the exposure to get folks back in here on a more regular basis. That will help the bottom line you're so anxious about. I'm counting on it to put us back in the black."

This shot down every objection that had occurred to Andrea. Molly was more concerned about the downturn in business than she was letting on. Andrea understood on a very basic level. Sometimes you had to do whatever it took to take care of your child, and to Molly, this pie shop was like a child. "All right, then. I promise I'll do my best to ensure the pilot is as entertaining as...*The Real Housewives of Kalispell*."

Molly's brows arched. "There is no such show. Oh, ha. I see. That's funny." They laughed. Then a familiar, determined gleam returned to Molly's eye. "Now let's work on getting you a husband. Hmm. Who would make a good candidate?"

"Oh, no you don't." Andrea raised her palms to ward off the very notion.

"Okay, I'll have to think on it anyway." Humming, Molly retreated to the kitchen.

Five minutes later, the bell over the door sounded, and Andrea turned toward it in anticipation of customers, but it was only Suzilynn, their part-time counter help, arriving after school. The pert brunette, whose ponytail reached to her waist, had a friendly demeanor, did as she was told, but was not a self-starter. Her eyes popped wide behind wire-rimmed glasses. "OMG. It smells like my grandpa's apple orchard in here, only a gazillion times sweeter."

"Molly's newest recipe."

"Maybe we should prop open the door to lure in some customers. This place is deader than my cell phone."

"It's early yet," Andrea said, trying to reassure herself as much as to counter any bad vibes that statement conjured.

"If Ms. McCoy would play rap music instead of country, I could get my friends to come in after school."

Andrea bit her tongue to keep from reminding the girl that Big Sky Pie was a pie shop, not a teenager hangout. "Or maybe you could suggest they bring in their families for dessert after dinner."

Suzilynn's mouth puckered as if it were full of vinegar. "Their families?"

Andrea gave up, feeling old for not relating to this teenager. Not that long ago, she'd been a teen, right? "Until someone comes in, you can keep busy refilling the sugar holders. I have to make a couple of phone calls."

"If someone does come in, should I get you?" Suzilynn pushed her glasses up her nose.

"Not unless it's a stampede. Just take orders and serve the desserts." Andrea stifled her frustration. Suzilynn was capable of handling the café alone as long as there were no more than two tables of customers at the same time. Andrea seriously doubted that would be a problem today.

As Andrea stepped into the kitchen, a sorrowful country tune issued from the CD player. The kitchen staff was gone, the last of the day's pies were cooling on the racks, and Molly was wiping down the work area to ready it for tomorrow, singing along, making up words she didn't know, her voice off-key. Sunlight shone in through the row of windows at the back wall and glinted off the stainless steel appliances. The cabinets were French Country, creamy and soothing, the large island workstation a solid slab of marble, its consistently cold surface the best for rolling pie dough.

Andrea made her calls, then came back out to find Molly finishing up. Molly handed her two pies. "These need to go out front. And I'm heading home."

"See you tomorrow." Andrea carried two pies to the display cases in the café. As she settled them onto a glass refrigerator shelf, she noted that in her absence a couple of men had arrived. *Good.* They sat in the middle of the three booths, conversing in low tones, viewing something on an iPad. The baby-faced one didn't seem much older than Suzilynn, a lanky, pink-cheeked kid, all legs and arms he had yet to grow into. The other guy was shorter, but well built, and surprisingly tan for someone with natural red hair. They were halfway through the specialty dessert à la mode.

Suzilynn had served them without mishap, Andrea was glad to see. Maybe all the girl needed was some confidence-building encouragement. She made a note to herself to offer praise whenever she could. She motioned for Suzilynn to see if the men needed more coffee. Suzilynn blushed, glanced at Baby Face, and caught his eye. His flirty, puppy-dog grin brought to mind Molly's words about the caramel apple pie.

Andrea shook her head, smiling to herself, and then she realized the redhead had focused on her. He said something she couldn't hear to his companion, and then both guys were glancing at her like they were auditioning the future mother of their children.

Andrea's spine stiffened. *As if.* Molly was wrong. She didn't need or want a husband. A man couldn't define her life or make it better. In fact, given her one and only foray into that not-so-happy state of matrimony, she'd rather avoid it forever. But was that fair to her two little boys? Mommy-guilt fell over her like a wet blanket. They had no man in their lives, no father figure, and there were just some roles a mom and grandma couldn't fulfill. For their sakes, shouldn't she try to find a guy who would make a wonderful stepfather? Didn't she owe them that?

Of course she did.

The bell over the café door jangled, announcing more customers, and before she could even glance up to greet the new arrivals, her bad-boy antennae began to twitch. A moment later, he filled the doorway, tall, blond, tan, with mirrored aviators and an unconscious swagger. Her knees went weak. *God help me.* He wore Harley boots, torn jeans, a leather jacket, and an I-don't-give-a-shit-about-anything attitude. Exactly her type. *Be still, my heart.* But that disobedient organ boogied inside her chest like a drunken line dancer, her pulse thrumming to the beat of an erotic guitar.

She braced herself and carried a menu to his table near the café's bay windows. "Welcome to Big Sky Pie. May I get you something to drink?"

"Depends," he said in a drawl that rivaled Sam Elliott's gravelly voice. He lifted his face, the lenses hiding his eyes. "What are you offering?"

Tingles rocked through Andrea, and she almost responded, "My body," but swallowed the words. "We have milk, coffee, espresso, tea, and water."

"Espresso." He rattled off some concoction with five ingredients.

Andrea laughed. "This isn't Starbucks. Our espresso is the basic brew."

"Then basic it is." His smile flashed teeth that were brighter than the porcelain sink in her apartment bathroom. Her gaze fell to his hands. No wedding ring. Not that that meant a thing. His kind never wore rings. She'd bet he was on a road trip, out for a good time with any and every female who crossed his path. No strings attached. Again, exactly her usual choice in lovers.

She swallowed hard as thoughts of making love with

this man began stirring sensuous images and heating her blood. She turned to get his drink, but he stopped her. "Andrea?"

She blinked, startled that he knew her name. Were those mirrored aviators hiding the eyes of a guy she actually knew? Not possible. She would remember someone this hot. Then she caught her reflection in the mirrored glasses, her teal sweater... her name tag. "Yes?"

"What is that delightful scent?"

"It's the special of the month, caramel apple pie." She pointed toward the chalkboard menu, debating whether or not to shake some of his cockiness by telling him what Molly thought men would do after eating one bite of this pie. She smiled to herself but, in the end, decided against it. He'd probably take off running, and they needed his business. "It tastes even better than it smells."

"I'm sure it does." He shared a crooked, sexy-as-hell grin. "But I meant your perfume."

Andrea rolled her eyes. Seriously? Did this line actually work for him? Hell—considering the sex appeal radiating off him—probably any line worked. "How could you smell anything but the yummy aromas coming from our kitchen?"

"I have a very discerning nose."

"I see." More likely she'd dumped on too much fragrance that morning in her haste to get the boys to school.

"It's Chanel, right?"

This brought her up short. Maybe he wasn't a low-brow Neanderthal after all. Most of the guys she dated couldn't decipher cologne from air freshener. The scent she wore was an old one, the bottle given to her mother and regifted to Andrea. Andrea seldom spent money on herself and never for luxury items like expensive perfume. The boys' needs came first. Always. "What are you? A perfume salesman?"

He chuckled and leaned back in the chair, looking her up and down. "No one's ever called me that before."

A slew of things he probably had been called popped to mind and made her smile. His corresponding grin said he'd like to eat her up, and her body responded with a "Hell, yes!" Rattled, she escaped to the coffee bar for his espresso.

Suzilynn pushed her glasses up her nose and whispered, "He's hot...for an old guy."

Hot and a half, Andrea thought, but acted as if she hadn't really noticed his eye-candy delightfulness. "You think?"

"Yeah, I think. Who is he?"

*A slick, smart-ass, Donnie Lovette clone.* She shrugged. "Dunno. Some Harley Cowboy, just passing through."

"Really?" Suzilynn's eyebrows rose above the frame of her glasses. "Then how come he's taking photos of the café and everything?"

Andrea glanced toward Mirrored Aviators and received another heart jolt. "I didn't see a camera."

"He was using his phone and texting." Suzilynn's eyes

rounded, a sure sign her imagination was about to run wild. "I bet he's some spy, checking out the competition."

"I doubt it." She dismissed the teenager's ridiculous suggestion and turned back to the espresso machine, reaching for his cup. But what if Suzilynn was on to something? Andrea shifted around quickly and caught him lowering his cell. A squiggle of unease wound through her. Could he be here scouting out this shop with plans to open something similar down the street in an attempt to run Molly out of business? On the surface, the idea seemed ludicrous, but given that receipts were dropping by the day, she couldn't shake it off. They were barely covering expenses.

"I'll find out." Suzilynn started toward Mirrored Aviators.

"No." Andrea caught her by the arm. "You can't just ask him."

"Why not?" The teenager gaped at her.

Andrea handed Suzilynn the espresso cup. "Take him this and get his pie order. And that's all."

Suzilynn was back a minute later. "He wants the special à la mode, but he wants you to deliver it."

*Of course he does.* She plated a slice of the caramel apple pie, heated it, then topped it with a scoop of cinnamon ice cream. The aroma snaked into her like erotic incense. Too bad its magical powers didn't include making a man tell the truth. She carried the dessert to his table.

She meant to ask if he needed anything else, but heard herself saying, "I know what you're doing."

"You do?" He seemed amused by the statement. "What gave me away?"

She raked a smoldering gaze the length of him, hoping to make him squirm. Like he'd made her squirm. "The way you're dressed, for one thing."

He glanced at his attire, then at her. "I don't get the connection."

"Oh, you get it."

"I do?"

The more amused he became, the more her anger spiked. "If you do anything to hurt Molly McCoy or this business, you'll have me to answer to."

He made a rumbling noise that sounded like suppressed laughter and that sparked hot shivers through her.

He said, "In that case, I won't do that."

"Make sure you don't."

He lifted his phone and snapped a photo of her. Andrea reared back, lost her balance, grabbed at air, and caught the tablecloth. As she pitched bottom-first to the floor, she watched the pie à la mode jump, then take flight, and drop into Mirrored Aviators' lap, the dish landing at his boots with a clatter. He swore, leaped from his chair, and cried, "Cut! Did you get that, Berg?"

"Of course I did." The redheaded dude slipped from the booth. "Wait 'til you see the footage. It's amazing."

Andrea, legs askew, skirt hiked up her thighs, realized she was giving these guys more than a little shot of her unmentionables. She scrambled to her feet, resisting the urge to rub her sore behind. "What the hell are you talking about?"

As Mirrored Aviators swiped at the front of his pants with a damp tea towel provided by Suzilynn, Berg pointed to the shelf beneath the chalk blackboard. Andrea's eyes widened. A camera. And another beside the cash register. Why had Suzilynn allowed that? She spun toward her counter girl to ask, but the teenager was cleaning up the mess and Baby Face was helping. Flirty glances and giggles passed between them. It was all the answer Andrea needed. He'd diverted Suzilynn so "Berg" could position the cameras.

Andrea's hands landed on her hips, murder filling her heart. She spun on Mirrored Aviators. "Who are you?"

He grinned and extended his card. "Ice Erikksen. My partner, Bobby Bergman. Ice Berg Productions. We're in charge of making the pilot for the reality show. And thanks to you, Andrea, we just got a sweet opening sequence."

# Chapter Two

Ice Erikksen leaned over the iPad, reviewing the video taken yesterday in the pie shop. He stalled the clip on the sexy blonde with the hard-on-inducing curves and legs that could welcome a man to Heaven. His body responded accordingly. He enlarged the image, the close-up shot of her hot ass, and grinned. "This place has definite appeal, Berg."

Bobby emerged from the bathroom wearing boxers and the pained expression of a man hungover. He glanced at the screen and sighed. "My wife would cut off my balls for the thoughts racing through your mind right now."

"That's why she's your ex," Ice said a little more harshly than he might have if her loss to Bobby had been a bad thing. But it was the smartest move his buddy had made in a long while. A social-climbing, world-class bitch, she'd set her sights on Ice first, wanting him for all the wrong reasons. When she realized that wasn't going to happen, she'd gone after Bobby, thinking he might be a means into Ice's inner circle. She didn't understand that Ice was an island, cut loose from all ties to his famous family, who had legally changed his name to keep him safe from fame-by-association seekers like her. Just thinking about her pissed him off. She was one more reason he was never getting married.

Not that he needed another reason.

What really bugged him, though, was how she'd discovered his true identity. He guarded that secret like the Colonel did his original chicken recipe. Bobby swore he hadn't been the leak, and Ice wanted to believe him... because if he found out that was a lie, this partnership was toast.

"What do you think?" Ice asked, leaning back in the suite chair, stocking-feet crossed at the ankles. He took a long drag of his favorite morning heart charge, a venti Caffè Mocha, grateful that Starbucks was everywhere—even in the uncivilized wilds of Montana.

Bobby rubbed the stubble on his chin, his bloodshot gaze shifting to Ice. "I think this is the least prepared we've ever been. No loglines, no script. Not even a rough outline."

"Yeah, well, having someone offer to sponsor the pilot negated any need for those things. And it gave me time to wrap up the final cut on *Bikini Barristas of Malibu*."

Bobby's grin was X-rated. "I really thought that was cash in the bank. Can't believe how fast studios have passed on it."

"Not all of them. ID TV is still considering."

"The Investigative Discovery channel?" Bobby plopped into the chair, tugging on jeans as rumpled as if he'd slept in them. He smirked. "Yeah, I suppose it's appropriate. There's a lot to investigate and discover."

Ice took another slug of coffee, welcoming the kick of caffeine. "Seriously, if sex doesn't sell, what do you think of the potential for this pilot now that you've seen Big Sky Pie?"

Bobby stood and zipped his fly, then dug in his duffle for a fresh T-shirt emblazoned with the Ice Berg Productions logo. "It's a great title for a reality show."

"That's true." Ice nodded. "And...redneck is the new black."

"Shit yes." Bobby sat back down and pulled on socks. "From Monster Hunters to Honey Boo Boo, and Duck Dynasty, why not a Montana pie shop?"

"What angle do you think we should take in the story?"

Bobby grew thoughtful. "I'm not sure. My main concern is that everyone we've met so far seems too... nice. 'Nice' don't sell."

"Ah, come on. Everyone is always on their best behavior when we first show up. That's why we didn't walk in and announce ourselves yesterday. I wanted to capture something genuine and unguarded."

"And boy, did we." Bobby tied the laces of his sneakers.

Ice glanced at the iPad screen again, at Andrea's enticing curves. "Their true colors will come out once we dig down to the bottom of the pot and give it a few good stirs. During the interviews today, see if you can figure out what the moral code is or should be, and who is following it, and who is breaking it."

"And who will make the most appealing villain."

The sexy blonde sprawled on the floor with her skirt hiked to her hips flashed through his mind. She hadn't apologized for dumping pie and ice cream on his jeans. Just given him a sassy glare. She might make a great villain. And a hell of a lot more.

The thought shocked him.

Ice pulled his gaze from her delightful image on his iPad, reminding himself of *Rule 1* in the reality series game: *No fraternizing with the cast.* That included making friends with benefits. Nope. That was a mistake he wouldn't repeat. As tempting as Andrea Lovette was, he'd rather pay for sex than deal with the complications of a relationship, even a temporary one.

*Rule 2: See Rule 1.*

People, he'd learned, were all the same. Rich or poor. Famous or unknown. They all wanted fame and money. Fame usually more than money. As if being a celebrity would make their lives better. He could tell them otherwise, but he knew they wouldn't believe him. *It is what it is.* A huge steaming pile of bullshit.

"You're doing it again, Erikksen."

"What?" Ice tossed a puzzled glance at Bobby.

"Sneering like a cynic."

"I'm just a realist."

He thought he caught a look of pity in his partner's eyes, but Bobby clapped him on the shoulder and grinned. "Nope." Bobby chortled. "You just need to get laid."

\* \* \*

Andrea leaned on the frame of the office door, taking a break from her bookkeeping, and listening to the kitchen staff chattering about their two favorite subjects. Guys and pies. Her own mind had been on one guy in particular since yesterday. Ice Erikksen. She made a face. The thought of the humiliation he'd handed her still rankled. A decent guy would have been up front about who he was. Just one more reason to dislike him.

And yet recalling that hot gaze that could melt the very thing he'd been named, she knew she didn't dislike him. A warm thrum stirred inside her. Without thinking, she blurted out, "Who names their son 'Ice' anyway?"

"There is no accounting for some mothers' tastes," Molly said, looking up from the Granny Smith apples she was slicing over a huge ceramic bowl. The bowl contained a mixture of sugar, nutmeg, salt, and cinnamon.

"He's from Los Angeles, the land of kids named after fruits and nuts." BiBi Hendersen, assistant pastry chef, glanced over her shoulder. A small, big-eyed brunette with a pixie haircut, she stood at the sink, peeling and coring green apples. A new tattoo glowed red at her wrist. A single word. *Defiance.* "I know. I grew up there."

"Nick and I won't be naming our child after a food item." Jane Wilson Taziano, head pastry chef and an artist with piecrusts, rolled a mound of dough to the perfect round, a task made harder every day by her advancing pregnancy. Pink flooded her face and spread into her strawberry blond roots as if she'd said something politically incorrect. "We're only considering normal family names."

Since Jane's mother's name was Rebel, Andrea couldn't help wondering just what Jane considered a normal family name. But she hadn't asked the question about Ice's name to criticize anyone. She hadn't meant to voice that question at all. It had just spilled out.

What was wrong with her that she was expending so much energy thinking about a man that she had no intention of getting to know beyond the filming of the pilot? He was the walking-one-night-stand kind of trouble she didn't want or need, but couldn't usually resist. Dread for today's meeting swam in her stomach.

"What time is Ice Berg Productions due to arrive this morning?" She tried to sound casual, but heard the tremor in her voice.

"Yeah," BiBi said, "I want my hair and makeup camera-ready. Or wait, are they bringing makeup and hair people for the filming? Does anyone know?"

Jane blushed. "I might have a doctor's appointment today. I need to check my schedule."

Andrea tensed. The film crew weren't even here yet and they were causing stress. She went to the pastry chef's side. Jane was shy. Having her pie-making skills praised was one thing, but a camera following her every move? A sure recipe for disaster. "It's going to be okay, Jane. Just be yourself and you won't have anything to worry about."

Jane peered up at her, a smudge of flour on her nose, looking anything but convinced. "What if I say something stupid? I don't want to embarrass Nick, or my folks."

"That's what editing is for," Molly said, setting aside the paring knife and reaching for a large wooden spoon. "I'll tell Mr. Erikksen and Mr. Bergman that we don't want anything in the pilot that reflects badly on one or the other of us. I'm sure they'll cooperate."

A choking sound issued from BiBi. Andrea's brows arched. Either their boss was getting high on the fumes of sugar and cinnamon as she stirred the finely sliced apples into the mixture, or she had just out-and-out lied—something as alien to Molly McCoy as dancing the tango in a country-western bar.

"Stupid is good for ratings," BiBi said, gathering the apple peelings into a garbage receptacle and then scrubbing the freshly skinned Granny Smiths. "Trust me, the more drama they can squeeze out of us, the better the chances are that some network bigwigs will option the show. Then we'll be lining our pockets with the kind of dough that I can spend on a new car."

Molly scowled at the assistant pastry chef as though

she'd like to find a roll of duct tape and seal her mouth shut. Andrea had had that same reaction herself, but this time, BiBi wasn't in the wrong. The conversation frayed her last nerve. She headed to the café for some coffee.

It was Monday, the usual "closed" day for the pie shop, and there were no customers. The pies being readied in the kitchen today were for a special order. The last of this month's special orders.

Worry crept through her as she filled a mug with coffee and added cream for the sake of her stomach. Her mind reeled. Would this Hollywood solution blow up in their faces like the crazy stunt that it was? Or would the pilot get sold and put the shop back in the black? And if it did, would the show change everyone's lives in ways that none of them expected? The latter was her biggest fear.

But Molly seemed intent on denying the chaos that reality shows thrived on, despite being a self-professed fan of the genre. She had to know that if this pilot was to sell to a network, it would need to include a lot of juicy gossip, snarky sound bites, and embarrassing moments—like the embarrassing moment she'd had yesterday spilling pie on Ice and landing on her behind.

She came into the kitchen as Molly was saying, "I plan for our reality show to be real, and to reflect the harmony in my pie shop, and to show that our delightful desserts bring the Montana community together in a family-friendly atmosphere."

"No offense, Ms. McCoy," BiBi said, "but this isn't an ad for Big Sky Pie."

"No, dear, but it can be."

BiBi glanced away, then back at Molly, her lips pursed in disbelief. "Well, then, I hope for your sake it doesn't turn out that they expect some nitty-gritty, redneck-female, back-stabbing bitchiness."

Molly's mouth snapped shut. Andrea knew she'd put all her eggs in this pilot basket, and the set of her shoulders said she didn't want to hear anything that hinted at what a huge mistake that might be. It spoke volumes, Andrea realized, about how worried she actually was over the falling receipts. Molly began filling the readied pans with the apple mixture she'd made, and Jane started rolling out the top crusts.

"I'll take that next batch of apples if they're ready, BiBi," Molly said. "You can help me make dumplings."

The chatter died off to a normal pie production discussion, measuring ingredients, rolling pin clicks, and soft music floating over the room from the CD player. Andrea returned to the closet-sized office. She sank onto the desk chair, sipping coffee, considering what she could do to help the shop's bottom line. An idea occurred to her. She closed QuickBooks and pulled up the special events folder on the computer. The few items stood out in bold lettering against a sea of empty calendar squares. Disheartening. But she found the best way to fight discouragement was with action. She read her notes on potential customers who'd consulted her in the past month, and her training in the real estate office kicked in. She had been the master of follow-up phone calls. She began jotting down numbers.

The noise level in the workroom suddenly amped up three octaves, like a crowd cheering at a football arena, sending a jolt through Andrea. She dropped her pen. It took another second to realize that Ice Berg Productions had arrived. She rose to shut the door, but Molly gestured for her to join them. With reluctance, she did.

Bobby Bergman looked as though he'd been rode hard and put away wet. His red hair hid beneath a Rams baseball cap, but even the shadow of its brim couldn't block the streaky redness in his eyes or the gray pallor of his tanned skin. Ice, however, sauntered in as cool as a winter breath. His magnetic gaze swept the room and landed on her. Andrea felt a flash jab through her, something like a fork of lightning—hot, electric, terrifying—rendering her weak-kneed and too aware of his gaze on her cleavage.

If she could blink herself home, she'd be back at her closet choosing something button-to-the-chin chaste to wear. Like a turtlenecked muumuu. *Is there such a thing?* She rubbed her hand down the second-skin jeans she'd loved at first try-on, wishing she'd chosen something in a dark, gloomy color to complement them instead of her sunny yellow sweater. The one with the too-low neckline that hugged the body she'd worked so hard to get back and maintain after having her second son.

She swallowed and mentally bitch-slapped herself. She wouldn't give a hoot that she was wearing this if some other guy, any guy but Ice Erikksen, was the one taking her measure. She could have opted for something

Amish just to keep him from glancing her way, but why should she change who she was for the sake of some guy who couldn't keep his sexy gaze to himself?

As Baby Face came through the back door, a ginormous camera on his shoulder, Ice said, "Flynn, I want some film of the staff putting these pies together."

"Sure." Flynn adjusted some of the wires that snaked down into a fanny pack around his waist. Someone else came in with a klieg light, and the room lit up as if the sun had burned away the roof. Everyone flinched like criminals about to be interrogated.

Andrea thought about going for her sunglasses.

As Flynn filmed, Ice assessed the women in the kitchen the same way old man Hooper did whenever he came in for a slice of rum raisin pie, first counting the raisins, then deciding if there was enough whipping cream, then making sure he wasn't cheated a millimeter shy of a full slice. Andrea squirmed under Ice's watchful eye. She sidled up to him, speaking softly. "What are you doing?"

He grinned down at her, the smile slow and not quite reaching his eyes. "Taking mental notes for my script."

*Script?* Hah. She knew it. These reality shows *were* scripted. And everyone wanted folks to believe they were slices of real life. "What is the script about?"

"Don't know. Haven't written it yet."

"Really. I thought that you had to pitch a story or two to a network before they'd pay for funding a pilot."

He raised an eyebrow, assessing her with a sensuous, raking glance. "What do you know about networks ordering pilots?"

"Nothing really." Nothing she hadn't researched on the Internet.

She glanced away, deflecting his allure with effort. Something about this guy spoke to her on a primal level as no man had done in years. And that rattled her.

"Every pilot is different," Ice said.

What did that mean? She'd done her homework, Googled and watched a series of YouTube videos on writing and selling a pilot to a studio. The writing process could be a couple of weeks long, but then you had to present a variety of different possible story lines to the studios and then wait for a response. That could take weeks more. Most times you were rejected. But if Ice's proposal hadn't been accepted, his production company wouldn't be here. "Which studio or network ordered the pilot?"

They stepped back out of Flynn's way as he maneuvered around the table to get a better shot of Jane plying her talents on the crust of one of the apple pies, every tweak of her little fingers producing as identical a crimp as the one before. Molly had moved to the sink with the big bowl. BiBi busied herself wiping down the surface of the marble counter that Molly had used and placing ready-to-bake pies into the ovens.

"Obviously some network is interested or you wouldn't be here. So which one is it?"

"I can't say right now."

His elusiveness twisted the nervous knot in Andrea's stomach. He sounded just like Donnie used to—half-truths and outright lies buried in avoidance. Was there even a studio attached to this project yet? Of course there was. There had to be, unless he was funding this pilot himself. And why would he do that? "Mr. Erikksen—"

"Ice." He looked as though nothing formal should stand between them, as though absolutely nothing should be between them, not even clothes.

Andrea felt fires starting up all through her body, tiny flames that threatened to turn her resolve to avoid this man into a pile of ashes. "What do you think the chances are that this show will be picked up?"

"Let's not get ahead of ourselves."

"What does that mean?"

"It means I can't answer that question when I don't have any film yet or any sound bites or anything else to base a response on."

"Oh."

"We'll be doing interviews in a few minutes. I want to speak to everyone first, though." He turned to Flynn. "That's enough for now."

Jane finished the last of the piecrusts, and BiBi stuck the pie in the oven, then set the timer. The used utensils and appliances were brought to the sink. The island was scrubbed.

Ice said, "Ladies, can we let those dirty dishes sit for a few minutes? I'd like to give you an idea of what we'll be doing today."

Everyone took a stool at the marble work island. One smile and he had their rapt attention, including Andrea's. Though she didn't much like it.

He said, "What we're needing from each of you is just something about yourself, why you're working here, what your goals are. What you think of the pie shop, the work, and your coworkers."

"The usual reality show stuff," Bobby said on a grin.

BiBi beamed at the redheaded man as if he were a screen god, not some hungover, bleary-eyed producer. "Oh, goodie. I love reality shows. Have you seen *RDOHM*?"

At their blank expressions, Jane said, "*The Real Daughters of Hollywood Moguls*?"

"Oh, yeah, Ice has a serious connection with that show." Bobby laughed, obviously dull-witted this morning. The comment earned him a nasty look from Ice and a determined-to-figure-out-the-connection glance from BiBi.

Andrea thought BiBi was going to swoon and fall off the stool, but somehow she managed only to give a squeal of delight. "That's my all-time favorite show. I DVR it, then watch it and watch it and rewatch it. My favorite regular is Ariel Whittendale. Her daddy owns iMagnus Studios. You've heard of him, right?"

Although BiBi was addressing Bobby, Andrea saw something dark pass through Ice's eyes at the question. He blinked, hiding it, and said with a cutting disinterest, "Yeah, we've heard of him."

But Andrea didn't care for the devious gleam that came into Bobby's eyes. She'd bet he was making some sort of mental note about BiBi, like she was auditioning for a role in a horror movie.

"So we're going to need to meet with each of you privately," Bobby said. "Who wants to be first?"

"I do." Molly raised her hand. "It's been a long day for this old bird, and I'd like to get it over and done with and go home for a nap."

"Sure." He moved her to a stool that didn't have the gleaming chrome appliances behind her, explaining that the glare would ruin the take.

Flynn repositioned a kleig light to shine almost directly on Molly. It was like some space monster sucking the color from the human skin. She took on a ghostly hue. "What about my hair and makeup?"

"We've hired Trula's Trendy Tresses."

BiBi's expression fell. "I thought you'd be bringing your own team from Hollywood."

Ice shook his head. "Wouldn't make much sense in a show set in Montana if you all ended up looking like you belonged in L.A."

"Don't worry, dear." Molly tugged off her apron, hand fluffing her hair. "Trula's been doing my hair since we were both in high school together."

BiBi muttered something that Andrea thought sounded like, "That's what I'm afraid of."

But it wasn't Trula who showed up. It was her daughter, Zoe, a rainbow-haired, facially pierced, dragon-tattooed, untidy nineteen-year-old. "Mama wanted this job more than anything, but these fellas picked me."

Andrea evil-eyed the men. Apparently their budget for this production was tight, but this was definitely a case of getting what you pay for. Zoe was still in beauty school. She wasn't a fully accredited hairdresser, just the shampooer at Trula's.

Zoe plunked a bag that looked like a cat carrier, hair and goo included, onto the marble work island. Molly gasped, her face going as white as the flour smudge on Jane's nose. "Get that filthy thing out of here."

For a second, Andrea thought she meant Zoe, but Molly meant the bag. Molly grabbed it by the handle, inadvertently swinging the "filthy thing" toward the counter that held a rack of cooled pies. Andrea leaped for the pies. Zoe scooted past her and around the island with Molly hot on her tail, admonishing her every step of the way, bumping her in the back with the bag. "You'll have the Health Department shutting me down, Zoe. Your mama raised you better than to set a germ-laden bag onto a kitchen counter."

"I'm sorry, Ms. McCoy."

As they headed for her again, Andrea hoisted two pies out of harm's way and spun toward the café. From the corner of her eye, she saw that Flynn had his camera on. No time to worry about that. *Just save the pies.* But something rammed her in the spine. Zoe's bag. Andrea pitched forward and felt her balance slipping, like the day before. She let out a squeal. Ice lunged to save her. Or at least the pies. Her grip on the pans cut loose. One caramel apple pie went airborne. Ice saw it coming and tried to scramble back, but the pie struck him just below the belt. He groaned, buckling over and landing on the floor.

Somehow, Andrea righted herself without stepping

on Ice or losing her grip on the other pie. She exchanged the pan with BiBi for a damp towel and then knelt beside Ice. "I'm sooo sorry. Are you okay?"

"You don't need to keep dumping pie on me," he said in a husky voice that only she could hear. The smoldering look in his eyes tightened her throat and loosened a need deep inside her. "If you want to get me out of my pants, sweetheart, all you need to do is ask."

# Chapter Three

~~~~~~

Dreaming about sexy men all night didn't usually result in Andrea waking up grouchy, but this morning, she could bite off the head of a grizzly without thinking twice. Damn Ice Erikksen and his insolent comments. He was a jerk. A card-carrying asscap.

She stared into her closet, uncertain what to wear, and realized the indecisiveness was a by-product of one horny Hollywood bad boy accusing her of lusting after him. Anger boiled in her stomach. She'd given him no reason to think that. Not a one. A twinge of guilt struck. Well, okay, maybe a longing gaze had flicked in his direction once or twice, but that was it. She hadn't brushed up against him or touched him on purpose or said anything that could be mistaken for an invitation into her bed. She'd dumped pie on him. That was not a come-on. In fact, most men would probably find it a total turnoff.

So what if she dressed a little seductively? It wasn't a crime. She wasn't dead. Or married. As they used to say on the rodeo circuit, it wasn't the age of the cowboy but his years in the saddle that counted. By that measure, she was ten years older than her actual twenty-five. And she'd never let any guy dictate her wardrobe. She wasn't about to start now. How she put her outfits together was the God-given right of every red-blooded American woman. A form of self-expression.

Then why was she still standing in her underwear staring at her closet? What was she looking at? *Cowgirl boots, denim shirts, and jeans. Stilettos, silk, and sweaters.* She grinned. There was no doubt about it. She was a whole lot of country with a bit of city thrown in for spice. While she'd worked for Molly's son managing his real estate office, she'd worn business attire, but the pie shop required dressing down, as if every day were Casual Friday. It suited her single-mom sensibilities much better and made getting ready every day easier.

Deciding to go with what she'd already laid out, she pulled on a sweater the same cocoa as her eyes, a knee-length denim skirt, and tan boots imbedded with turquoise accents. She glanced at the clock, prayed the boys were finished eating, and hurriedly brushed her hair into a ponytail, finishing up with a pair of turquoise and copper hoop earrings her dad had given her on her sixteenth birthday.

She did a quick inspection in her mirror. Was it in or out of fashion this year to wear eye shadow during the day? "Mom!"

The call to action jarred her out of the reverie. *So much for me-time.* She switched off lights as she made her way into the hallway of the three-bedroom apartment. The place wasn't large or new, but she had her own en suite bathroom, and for a mother of two boys, that was a luxury she felt blessed to have found. The cry came at her again just as she reached the tiny kitchen and disaster.

"Lucas spilled the milk, and now I don't have any for my cereal," eight-year-old Logan lamented, adopting a disgusted big brother face, despite being only sixteen months older than Lucas. Lately he'd been showing more and more disapproval toward his younger sibling. It was a trend that worried Andrea, and she wasn't sure how to curb it.

The kitchen had a single bank of cabinets, faded yellow appliances, and just enough room for one small rectangular table shoved against the wall. All three chairs were pushed out as if they'd leapt back to avoid getting splashed. A carton lay overturned on its side, its contents spread across the oak surface like a snowy oil slick. Milk had seeped between the center crack and was drip, drip, dripping to the floor, with a larger river about to roll off the edge.

She grabbed a paper towel to stem the tide.

"I didn't mean to spill it, Mama," Lucas said, head hanging, eyes full of self-recrimination. He hated messing up anything. "I tripped."

"Spilled milk can be cleaned up," Andrea said.

"Yeah, but I got it all over me," he said, his voice so sad it broke her heart.

One glance at his splattered shirt and damp pants, and her mind immediately flashed to the shot of Ice Erikksen with pie all over his fly. Her cranky meter began to buzz again. She didn't dump pie on customers. Or on anyone. And yet she'd done it twice in as many days to the same man.

Maybe her childhood klutziness was resurfacing.

She righted the carton, realizing it was definitely empty now as she ruffled Lucas's thick blond hair and smirked. "Looks like you've inherited Mama's clumsy gene, pal."

Lucas shook his head, dismayed. "I don't want it."

She laughed. "I don't blame you. Now hurry up and change your clothes while I mop this up." He nodded. She called after him, "Put those wet things in the hamper."

"I will."

"But I didn't eat, and now there's no milk," Logan said, storm clouds in blue eyes that were the image of his dad's. He held his bowl of dry cereal to his chest, his expression implying this was her fault for giving him such a pain of a younger brother.

"You used to spill milk, too, buddy. It happens. You don't need to be so hard on him."

His mouth took on Donnie's selfish curl, and she cringed, thinking of other traits of his father's he might have inherited, like Donnie's reckless bent. He whined, "I'm hungry."

*And as cranky as me obviously.* "I'll tell you what, we'll do breakfast out today."

"Okay," he said sullenly, but she caught the quick smile in his eyes.

Fast food was a special treat that she gifted her sons only two or three times a year. God knew, she wasn't much of a cook beyond pretty basic fare, but with the exception of pizza twice a month, she tried to make sure the boys' diet was healthy.

As Logan poured his cereal back into its box, she swabbed up the spilled milk with paper towels and then gave everything a quick scrub with disinfectant cleanser.

"I'm ready," Lucas announced. He wore a clean T-shirt and jeans, his blond hair sticking up like a haystack.

"Run the comb through your hair. Hurry. We're gonna be late."

"No," Lucas said. "I don't like being late."

Andrea bit back a smile. Stressing about being late wasn't a great trait in a kid who had no control over the aspect of time in his life, but she figured it would serve him well as an adult and tried to accommodate him as much as possible. Today it was impossible.

Single-mommy guilt sped through her, along with an unbidden longing for someone to share the weight of raising her two precious sons.

*       *       *

*"What the hell is wrong with me?"* Ice smoothed his hand over his short, coarse hair, twisting his neck from side to side. In this predawn hour, his favorite time for

writing, he had the main room of the hotel suite to himself. The muted snores stealing through Bobby's closed door sounded like the frantic crash of the ocean at his Malibu beach house, but noise-squelching earphones shut out the distraction. A John Legend favorite lulled his muse. He should be writing full blast right now, but he couldn't get a handle on the script for this pilot.

The problem was Andrea Lovette. She kept invading his thoughts. He'd tossed and turned all night, his dreams one sexual adventure after another with her in the lead role. Damn. It was nuts. She wasn't even his type. Too curvy, too in-his-face, too kiss-my-ass. *Too much like me. It takes one to know one.*

But that wasn't all. Whenever their eyes met, he felt a shift in his equilibrium, as though the ground had cracked open beneath his feet, leaving him with a sense of standing on two halves of a chasm. If he wasn't careful, he might fall into the abyss. Probably explained why they'd landed on the floor twice since they'd met. He grinned, recalling her reaction to his offer of sex. Damn, he couldn't deny he'd wanted her then, and if they'd been alone, he might have acted on that baser instinct.

The idea had him smiling harder. His usual method of ridding himself of a brown-eyed, blond distraction like this was a tumble in the sack. Or two. But he'd learned the hard way what a disaster that could be. *Rule 1: No fraternizing with the cast.*

Determined to stop being sidetracked, he directed his attention to the individual interviews they'd shot yesterday, hoping for some juicy tidbits to kick-start his recalcitrant muse. The still unwritten script plagued him. He tapped the tip of a pen against the fresh legal pad that he preferred for taking notes, his gaze locked on the iPad screen. Molly McCoy's segment ran before his eyes, her voice spilling into his earphones, but instead of the perky redheaded shop owner, Ice kept seeing Andrea, hearing Andrea.

There was just something about her—a hunger deep in those alluring brown eyes that echoed a secret yearning buried in his soul. He reached for a bottle of water. Was she single, married, engaged? Involved? She didn't wear a wedding ring, but there might be a boyfriend, or a fiancé. The possibility prickled. He stretched, trying to shake off the irrational annoyance, and swore out loud. If he wasn't careful, she could get under his skin, but he *was* careful. Steel encased his heart. He hadn't earned the nickname *cold bastard* for nothing.

\* \* \*

The cool, gray day did nothing to soothe Andrea's nerves. She dreaded going into work, still embarrassed and pissed off, and not sure she could rein in those feelings enough to behave like a grown-up around Ice today, but there was a staff meeting, and not showing up was out of the question. She entered the back door of the pie shop, inhaling the delightful spicy and fruity scents, finding her bearings in the familiar. She ditched her purse and jacket in the cupboard, acknowledging her coworkers' warm greetings with one of her own.

A sweeping glance confirmed her suspicion that Zoe was running late as usual. Molly, BiBi, and Jane weren't fluffed or painted, but they each wore an apron and looked ready for work. She said a second silent "thank-you" for the absence of Flynn and his camera. But Ice and Bobby were also present, and her stomach squeezed, making her wish she'd skipped the greasy sausage and egg muffin she'd downed as she drove the boys to school.

Deciding she needed more caffeine to deal with whatever this day held in store, she went for coffee, bringing her cup to the work counter, where everyone was already seated. The only remaining stool put her directly across from the man of her nightmares. She refused to meet his mesmerizing gaze, concentrating instead on Molly to her left, on her coffee, looking anywhere that wasn't at Ice—a task made near-impossible by his neon orange, "look at me" surfer shirt.

Bobby called the meeting to order, and Andrea sat a little straighter. His eyes no longer had the lost-weekend redness, but his wrinkled shirt and crinkled face roused an image of Lucas after a night camping in a sleeping bag. If she didn't know they were booked at The Outlaw Inn, she'd think he was sleeping in his van. Then again, maybe he was innately sloppy like Logan's art teacher, who didn't see much beyond his own vision of the world.

"We're going to finish up the interviews today," Bobby said, pulling Andrea back to the matter at hand. She hoped she hadn't missed anything important but figured that, if she had, she'd discover it soon enough.

Bobby glanced at his phone like someone expecting an important call or text, but she suspected he had a checklist app of items he meant to discuss. "Oh," he said, "Zoe will be here soon to do hair and makeup. We'll also be filming while you go about your daily work routines, but there's no need for anxiety. Just be yourselves."

"And pretend they aren't capturing our every move on film," Molly whispered.

"Yeah, good luck with that." Andrea almost laughed. She didn't bother to remind her boss that this was what she'd signed them up for. She took a swig of coffee, only half listening to Bobby, deciding she would spend as much time as she could in the office, out of the camera's ever-watchful eye. She would also steer clear of Ice and pie.

Ice's rumbling Sam Elliott voice pulled her gaze to him. "Once we have a story script, we're going to need one of you to be the overall, on-screen spokesperson." He stared pointedly at Molly.

She heard Molly suck in a breath. "Oh, no, I can't do that. I'm sorry. I get flustered too easily since my surgery."

"Okay." Ice gave her a sympathetic, understanding nod, then looked at Jane next, his brilliant smile flashing like a spotlight. "How about our other head pastry chef?"

Jane blushed crimson to her strawberry blond roots, her eyes aghast with a horror that suggested she'd just been told the world had run out of flour. "No . . . I . . . no."

"Well, I'd love to do it," BiBi announced, leaning toward Ice, eager-eyed as a schoolkid with her hand raised, muttering, "Me, me, pick me."

Molly cleared her throat. "Andrea will do it."

Andrea froze, so surprised she momentarily lost her voice.

"But my daddy—" BiBi started, about to tell them all again that her father had once had his own TV show on the Food Network.

"Andrea's run a real estate office," Molly cut her off, "and held her own in tense situations."

"But I—" BiBi started again, hurt dancing in her round blue eyes.

"Andrea stays levelheaded in most every situation," Molly insisted. "She'll be perfect."

Steam seemed to billow from BiBi's ears like a pressure cooker about to explode. "Andrea lost her cool and dumped pie all over our director twice in two days."

"And she handled both times with grace," Molly said.

*No I didn't.* Andrea blanched, heat flooding her face a second later as she sat there too stunned to respond. She wanted to remind them both that she was sitting right here and to stop talking for her, but she might as well have laryngitis.

"That's settled then," Molly said with a finality that brought BiBi's mouth together tighter than a zipline.

Andrea wanted to say, "*I won't do it.*" It sounded like a responsibility she hadn't the time or the desire to take on. But the air already crackled with the kind of tension that just needed a spark to ignite so she held her tongue, toying with a hoop earring and trying to figure out how to placate BiBi. And now she was stuck working with Ice. *No good deed goes unpunished. This is my reward for promising to do whatever I can to ensure the TV pilot's success.*

"So, BiBi," Bobby said, "we'll do your interview first this morning."

BiBi perked right up, but the glint in her eyes sent a shiver down Andrea's spine. *No telling what she'll say, given how pissed off she is.*

As the thought occurred to her, Andrea caught Bobby and Ice exchanging an almost imperceptible look of glee. BiBi's resentment was the drama they thrived on, the emotional element that made their pilots sell. Andrea moved into the office, worry tracking her steps. Her own interview was scheduled for sometime today, and she could only imagine what kind of drama they might drag out of her. She wished she could avoid it. She'd already played the fool twice on camera in the past two days.

She spent the next two hours ignoring everything beyond the office door, engrossed in bookkeeping and follow-up calls to potential bookings.

"Molly!" The high-pitched alarm in BiBi's voice brought Andrea to her feet. She hustled into the kitchen, visions of the day Molly had collapsed in this room racing through her head. But Molly stood near the ovens, looking as startled and clueless as Andrea felt.

"Molly!" BiBi's voice came again from the hallway.

They met her coming out of the cold room, her Crocs awash in dark liquid. She was juggling a dripping cloth as she raced toward the sink. "Something's wrong with the storage freezer. It's gushing like a chocolate fountain."

# Chapter Four

~⌒~

What are you talking about?" Andrea demanded, but the words *freezer* and *gushing* in the same sentence could only mean one thing. Bad news. Alarm did another turn through her system, slamming home a variety of possible calamities that losing the freezer could mean for upcoming events.

"The big freezer in the cold room is sitting in a puddle of goo," BiBi said, wrenching on the faucet as she plopped the saturated purple cloth into the deep work sink. She leaned toward the rag and sniffed, wrinkling her nose in disgust. "Smells like rancid fruit juice."

"Oh, no." Molly scooted past BiBi, hurrying down the hall. Andrea dogged her steps, a sinking feeling in the pit of her stomach.

Molly muttered, "I knew I should have bought a new

freezer, but that darned Charlie Mercer swore this one was refurbished and would outlast the newer models."

"Maybe it's not as bad as BiBi thinks," Andrea said, trying to calm her boss, not liking the high scarlet of her cheeks. Logically, she realized Molly probably wasn't having heart issues, just that she was heartsick about the possible loss of produce, but despite all the reassurances that the spritely redhead was doing great, Andrea couldn't stop worrying about her. She supposed it came from how close Molly had come to dying, a reminder Andrea hadn't needed of how suddenly life could end.

She shook off the thought and realized that, with every step, Molly was bawling herself out. "Why did I listen to Charlie? Jimmy used to say that man could sell bullshit to a cow, and still this old cow fell for a freezer-full of his steaming lies."

"I'll deal with Charlie Mercer," Andrea assured her. Part of her job description included handling salespeople and warranties. "Plus, you have insurance that covers the large appliances and loss of perishable inventory."

"Insurance can't replace fresh-frozen fruit from this past summer. I was counting on that to get us through the winter."

Andrea shut her mouth. Not being a chef, she looked at the fruit as a necessary tool of their trade, a commodity that could be replaced if something like this occurred, like the spilled milk this morning. To Molly, however, fruit was the paint for her artistic talent, the thing that took her pies from ordinary to extraordinary. The quality of the fruit was all-important, not to mention the hours of hard work that would be lost. She didn't want solutions. She wanted it not to be true.

Molly charged into the cold room first, banging the door against the wall. The space was large, filled with rows of racks with adjustable shelves that held apples, canned goods, and other supplies needed for making pies. A second Sub-Zero took up one wall, and the freezer hugged the opposite wall.

The windowless room was mostly kept in the dark, but the overhead lights were brilliant. Andrea blinked several times as she followed Molly, barely registering the cool temperature. Her attention was riveted on the massive white appliance that stood like a mound of dirty snow in one corner, a tall, upended ice fort that seemed to be melting into a pool of inky liquid.

"Holy crap," Molly said on a moan as she tiptoed through the puddle and yanked the door open. A gush of juice spilled out, followed by a couple of small, plastic-wrapped packets that cart-wheeled through the air and landed in the liquid, splashing her Crocs and pant legs. Molly let loose a string of profanities that would make a sailor blush, leaping back, slipping on the wet floor.

Andrea caught her from behind, keeping her upright.

Molly shook her off. "I'm okay, dear, but I might need to be bailed out of jail later today for doing bodily harm, or worse, to one fast-talking, jackass appliance dealer."

BiBi arrived with a bucket and mop. Andrea took them, and Molly sent BiBi back for a large trash container. Molly continued ranting as Andrea swabbed the floor directly in front of the freezer, getting the majority of the liquid, but leaving a smeary, purplish stain on the concrete.

The second she finished, Molly stepped to the freezer and plucked up a limp, drippy package of berries like she might a mouse by its tail, examining it from every angle, shaking her head in disgust. "It's what I feared. Warm. Ruined. All of it. The freezer has either been out for days or slowly giving up the ghost."

"Why didn't anyone notice?" Andrea asked, moving the mop to one side.

BiBi returned with two large, lined garbage pails.

"We aren't doing frozen berry pies yet." Molly dropped the package she'd been examining into the closest can, then continued doing the same, clearing the freezer shelves. Cherries, strawberries, blackberries, marionberries, and blueberries.

Andrea thought she heard a soft sob, but from the angle of Molly's chin and the ramrod set of her spine, she decided she'd imagined it. Although she felt like crying herself.

"Man, this sucks," BiBi said, hoisting a full pail, her face expressing the same pain as Molly's. "All the hours we spent cleaning and prepping this fruit..."

Andrea had no words to console either woman. She did the books and ran the café. She didn't work in the kitchen, hadn't had any part in preparing the packages now being tossed away, and yet her heart was just as heavy over this loss.

Her first instinct, however, was always to figure out how to fix a problem, not to wallow in the aftermath. That probably went back to those helpless teenage years when her mom was so ill. What she could do about this was contact their insurance agent to get the ball rolling on minimizing the dollar damage. That might not make Molly feel good at the moment, but it would help once she'd calmed down.

A noise behind her brought Andrea shifting toward the row of shelving. She half expected to find that Jane had joined them, but there was no one. And then a movement between the rows of shelving caught her eye. Flynn, camera to shoulder, was filming the whole mess. How long had he been standing there?

He noticed her glaring at him and waved his hand. "Just keep doing what you're doing. This is great stuff, ladies. Pretend I'm not here. We'll do some sound bites later."

No one kept doing what they were doing. Instead, everyone froze, staring at him. He lowered the lens, and Bobby popped up behind him. "Cut. Darn it."

"How long have you two been standing there?" Molly asked. If looks could kill, hers would have Bobby and Flynn staggering into the shelves and dying slow deaths.

A bead of suspicion rolled around in Andrea's head a few times before it clicked. She glanced at the freezer, curious as hell suddenly about what exactly had happened. Had it died of natural causes? Or had it been…murdered? Just how far would these guys go to create drama if none was occurring organically?

And where was Ice? Nothing happened without his hand guiding the wheel of this TV pilot.

"Well, here's some real-life drama for you," Molly said, anger in every word. Flynn's camera flew to his shoulder, its green light glowing. "We've lost all of the blueberries for Dean and Betty Gardener's wedding reception."

"Oh, no." Andrea sagged at this news. The reception was two weeks away, the biggest of their upcoming events. Dean and Betty owned a local floral shop, The Flower Garden, and their love story had touched everyone in the pie shop. They'd wanted to marry as soon as they finished school, but their parents took steps to ensure that didn't happen. Betty was sent away, and Dean joined the army. For several years, he was thought to have been killed in action, but he'd been captured and imprisoned. By the time he returned to the states, Betty was married to someone else, expecting her second child. When they finally found one another again, they eloped. But now they wanted to celebrate their marriage with family and friends, and Andrea wanted to make their special day perfect for them, and for Big Sky Pie. She felt sick. "Dean and Betty have themed the party around those blueberry pies. Blue flowers, blue tablecloths, centerpieces, outfits."

This was a major fail.

"You'll need to call the Gardeners," Molly said,

"explain what happened, and reassure them that we'll fix it somehow, but there is no way we can do blueberries or blackberries or strawberries now."

"Seriously," BiBi said, "it's not like this is anyone's fault. Shit happens, you know? I'm sure they'll understand once you explain it."

Andrea nodded, but she didn't share the assistant pastry chef's confidence. This celebration was too many years delayed for anything to go awry. She wouldn't blame Dean and Betty if they were too upset to trust Big Sky Pie to find a substitute. What if they hired someone else instead? Word would get around. The shop's reputation was at stake. Damn.

She didn't voice her concerns, but she feared Flynn and his camera had caught the worried expression that flashed across her face. He might look young, but that didn't mean he was naïve or innocent. He filmed reality shows for a living. And she realized that she'd be a fool to underestimate just how good he was at his job.

The question of how good niggled again. Had the young man tampered with the freezer? She scooted past Molly, seeking the wall outlet, needing to know whether or not someone had unplugged the cord. Disappointment jabbed through her. It was plugged in. And the "on" switch was activated inside the unit. But the walls and shelves were warmer than room temperature.

Another thought occurred to her. Unplugging the appliance would point directly to someone being guilty of causing this calamity. How else could a freezer be disabled? Do something to the motor? Sure, but then one of the kitchen staff might have realized it wasn't running while they were in here getting apples. So what then?

She caught up with BiBi at the outside disposal area. "How did Flynn and Bobby know to be in the cold room to film the cleanup at the freezer?"

Guilt crossed BiBi's face, quickly followed by a defiant set to her jaw. "My dad used to have his own TV show. I know what makes good TV. When I noticed the mess around the freezer—"

"You told them before letting Molly or me know," Andrea finished for her.

"So what if I did? You want this pilot to sell, right?"

Andrea couldn't deny that. She bit back the urge to read the assistant pastry chef the riot act. Going through proper channels wouldn't have changed the outcome. The freezer was already dead, the fruit already ruined. And starting an argument with BiBi would only fan the fire between them. "Did you notice either of them, or Ice, in or around the cold room in the past couple of days?"

BiBi frowned as she considered the question. "You think one of them did something to the freezer to make it stop working?"

Andrea shrugged, not hiding the suspicion she felt.

BiBi's eyes were silver-dollar rounds. "Why would they do that?"

"For exactly the same reason you told them before you told Molly about the freezer."

BiBi gasped. She leaned closer, her words conspiratorial now. "I see. Uh, I did see Ice and Flynn coming out of there the other day, but they said they were just doing interior shots. So I didn't think anything more about it. Is there some way to prove they did something to the freezer? I mean, if they did?"

"I don't know. But for now, let's keep this between you and me. Okay?"

"Of course." She ran her finger and thumb across her mouth. "My lips are zipped."

Andrea wasn't sure she believed that, but she nodded as though she did. She left BiBi to the cleanup task and headed to the office to call Betty and Dean Gardener, uncertain how to break the news. As she looked up their number, she began to wonder whether or not Freon could be drained from a freezer. She supposed Charlie Mercer could answer that. She looked up his number and dialed.

* * *

*Digital technology is sick*, Ice thought as he watched the video coming through from Big Sky Pie. *Greatest invention since sliced…pie.* He could view all the action from his hotel room without stepping foot on-site, and all of it was fodder for his script. If they couldn't get the employees and owners of the shop to bare their claws or expose their flaws, then they'd use any little disaster they could to create audience interest and ensure a following. The repercussions from the failed freezer and loss of the frozen fruit were gold in their pockets.

Network execs only cared about getting sponsors and viewers. Therefore, the content they presented them had to be guaranteed to snag viewers' long-term interest. And the emotion Flynn had captured in this sequence gave them a real shot at selling this pilot.

If they ever actually got a pilot rolling.

So far it was bits and pieces that needed editing and splicing together for the most entertainment value. Berg excelled at choosing the most titillating clips to splice together. The camera swept across the women as they emptied out the freezer, the dialogue compelling, the expressions on Molly and BiBi's faces pity-inducing. It was perfect.

But when *her* face filled the screen, Ice froze. Andrea. A walking wet dream. His body responded accordingly, blood flooding into his groin, desire stoking his hunger. The video offered a full body shot, and his gaze tracked over the long legs in patterned cowgirl boots, the hem of her skirt short enough to tease his imagination. And make him harder. Damn. His breathing caught and accelerated, and he realized, more than anything, he wanted a piece of that.

The lens moved in, focused on her face, on that incredible mouth, those intelligent eyes. She seemed to be staring directly at him. For a second, it disconcerted him, but then he understood. She'd realized Berg and Flynn were there, filming the freezer debacle. Her expression said this was not a nice surprise.

Ice grinned. She wasn't a pushover like that kid BiBi. This woman had been around the block. She would be a handful, and that tantalized. Andrea stared pointedly at the camera, then at the freezer, then back at the camera…a narrow-eyed suspicion spreading through her gorgeous brown eyes. In that instance, it felt as though she were reaching through the lens to grab hold of him by the neck.

That don't-mess-with-me glint lighting her gaze belonged to a wildcat. Damn, but he'd bet she could scratch it up in bed. No holds barred. Fantasies romped through his head as he dropped his legs onto the ottoman, lifted the Starbucks container of his favorite hot beverage off the end table, and raised it like a toast toward the screen now frozen on Andrea's image. He imagined her hands on his neck, his face, and destinations farther south. "Any time, sweetheart, just come and get me."

His cell rang, disrupting the erotic daydream. He let out a disappointed breath, struggling to get his mind and body back on business. *Private number.* He frowned. In his world, that could mean a lot of different callers, not all of whom he cared to speak with. He stared at the screen, debating whether to answer or delete the call. *Let them leave a message.* Then he'd call back if he wanted or needed to. Otherwise, he wasn't available.

He focused again on the laptop monitor, but the second he did, the phone buzzed. A text this time. He grabbed the phone. The sender's name was obviously a phony. Mick E Mouse. But it belonged to their silent partner, the anonymous benefactor footing the bill for the TV pilot. He—or she—wanted an update on the progress.

Ice worked the digital keyboard, giving a stock answer:

Early stages yet. Still establishing the story.
Gathering as much footage as we can.

Silent Partner texted back:

There's a bonus in it for Ice Berg Productions if the assistant pastry chef ends up with a prominent role.

*BiBi Henderson?* Ice considered the tiny brunette with the big blue eyes. Cute. Sexy in an obvious way, and he had to admit she'd been pivotal in Flynn and Bobby's filming the discovery of the dead freezer today, and the personal interview she'd given—after Molly declared Andrea would be the pie shop spokesperson— had mega-potential for drama. She was easily riled, liked being on camera, and didn't seem to have a filter. All good traits in an antagonist. She could very well be the one who bucked the moral code.

Ice texted:

Will take that under consideration. Thanks for the suggestion.

Bobby might jump on the offer of a bonus if it were big enough, given his recent divorce woes, but not Ice. He'd grown up rich, and unhappy. There wasn't anything he wanted that money could buy. Besides, he didn't like being told what to film. Or who. He liked the story to come about organically whenever possible.

As he started to set the phone aside, he noticed he'd missed a call from Quint McCoy. He supposed Molly's son also wanted to be briefed. Ice rang the number.

"Sorry I missed your call," he said when Quint answered. He didn't wait to be asked for the update. "There's nothing to report yet. We're just shooting a lot of footage and getting the script together, now that we've seen how the shop operates and observed which roles within that framework the staff plays."

"I don't know anything about how you work," Quint said on a laugh. "It's all Greek to me. I'll trust you to do what you do. As long as Mama is happy, Callee and I are happy, too. I just thought maybe you'd like a day off. Do some fly-fishing on the local river before the season is over. It would just be you, me, Jane's husband Nick, and one other guy."

Ice hadn't expected this offer, and it left him speechless. He'd met Quint and Nick when they were in Los Angeles a couple of months back, had taken them to a local sports bar to watch a Dodgers game and enjoyed their company. But fishing? A memory flooded through him, warming him. Poppy Erikksen, his mother's father, used to take him fishing whenever his parents were off shooting movies, but Poppy had ended up with Alzheimer's the same year Ice was sent to boarding school. Normally, Ice would turn down an offer like this. Hell, he should turn it down. He hadn't had a pole in his hand since. But he found himself saying he'd think about it.

But once he disconnected, the warmth of the memory faded immediately. Maybe his teenage years would have been different if his grandfather hadn't died. He shoved the thought away and reached for his laptop. As he rewatched the scene in the cold room, he picked up on the name of the couple who'd been counting on blueberry pies for their wedding reception. Betty and Dean Gardener. He wrote their names on his legal pad, underlined them, and added a huge question mark.

This was an angle they needed to follow up on. He didn't want Andrea meeting with them without Flynn and him there. The fact that their plans might be ruined was exactly the kind of sentimental shit audiences ate up. Their angst, their upset, and how they worked things out had universal appeal. How many wedding or other life-event celebrations ever ran one hundred percent smoothly? None. It was the stuff people texted and tweeted about.

The more he considered the possible consequences for the pie shop, the more he sensed great story material. What if Dean and Betty weren't so understanding? What if they decided to fire Big Sky Pie? He supposed it could happen. Drama. Lots of drama. All of it relatable to viewers.

Of course, this meant he'd be working one-on-one with Andrea. Now all he had to do was figure out some way to keep his hands off her. Damn. He tossed back a slug of coffee and felt the burn down his throat and through his middle, but it did nothing to cool his racing jets.

He had to quit thinking about her. She'd screw up

this whole deal if he didn't. The worst thing he could do was sleep with her, but he wanted to do the worst thing so bad his balls were turning blue.

A knock on the door startled Ice. He hadn't ordered room service and wasn't expecting anyone. He wore a pair of worn jeans and nothing else. Maybe Berg had forgotten his key. He went to the door, peered through the peephole, but whoever it was had it covered. He yanked open the door, pissed, not caring who it was or if his state of undress shocked. He didn't like unexpected visitors. "Listen, jerk-off—"

The next word froze on his tongue.

"I could say the same to you." Andrea moved toward him so aggressively that he reflexively retreated. She came into the room, looking a little disheveled and somehow sexier than she had at the morning meeting. Her Chanel scent drifted around him and into him, stirring another pleasant memory from his childhood. So much had happened to wipe out those pleasant recollections that he sometimes forgot there had ever been a happy time for him as a kid. But she brought back those moments and threw him off balance.

"Can you spare a few minutes?" Her tone took the question out of it.

"For you?" He'd gladly spare her more than a few minutes. Hours, if she wanted.

"Maybe you should put on a shirt?"

He touched his naked chest and raked her with his eyes from her boot tips to her pile of sexy blond hair. "Naw, I'm fine."

# Chapter Five

Ice was *fine*, all right, Andrea thought, swallowing the lump in her throat. *The finest male specimen this side of Big Mountain.* He might be okay wearing nothing but some faded, torn blue jeans, but she wanted him covered. All that broad, well-defined chest with its smattering of golden hair that glistened like silk, tempting her to touch. Her gaze fell to the trail of tawny fur that ran down the middle of the flattest stomach she'd ever seen in person—and she'd seen some tight male bodies—although she couldn't recall any guy that made her imagination and curiosity run so wild. Or one that made her ache to feel his rippled, tan flesh as much as she yearned to do at this moment. "Please, just put on a shirt."

He had her blocked between the door and the suite,

that I-don't-give-a-shit attitude evident in his spread-legged stance and the implacable set of his thick jaw. Without uttering a word, he seemed to be telling her, "I wasn't expecting company. You barged into my hotel suite. Take me as you find me."

And she wanted to take him, to squelch the desire that had been haunting her sleeping and waking hours since the moment she'd laid eyes on him. What was it about him, this blue-eyed demon, radiating a sexuality and desire that spoke to every cell in her body? Sensuous tremors rocked through Andrea. She wasn't some naïve schoolgirl. She'd seen her share of men in nothing but their pants—in nothing at all—but this didn't feel like any of those other times. This felt like her first time—as if she were a trembling virgin.

He leaned down as if for a kiss. "What can I do to you?"

*To?* Had he actually said *to*, not *for*? Another tremor skittered through her, and myriad things she'd like him to do to her sprang to mind. Touch her. Kiss her. Touch her some more. She swallowed, but her mouth wouldn't stop watering. In fact, she felt wet everywhere—hot and wet—as if she were standing in a steam bath. As if she were a steam bath.

He leaned even closer, those enticing lips grazing hers. "Andrea?"

His breath rushed into her mouth, warm and minty, mixed with espresso and a hint of mocha. Tingles raced the length of her. If she moved, they'd be kissing. She moved.

Their lips collided like something akin to lighting a fuse. She swore she heard a sizzle, felt a crackle of electricity, and then a jolt like a high wind crashing through power lines, sparks flying around and through her.

Ice moaned like a man finding relief for his agony. He grabbed her, gathered her close, closer, crushing her palms against the heat of his naked chest. Beneath her fingertips, his heart thundered, matching the native drumbeat of her own. Her breath grew quick and shallow, her skin seemed to flame at his every caress, and need coiled in her with the speed of light.

The world dissolved into sensation; nothing existed but the thrill of discovery. Andrea slipped her hands over sinew and muscles, across the hard surface of his taut stomach, creeping lower and lower to the waistband of his jeans. Ice growled sexily as her fingers popped the top button of his fly, and then the next, and slid inside to grasp his throbbing member.

He nibbled a trail from her lips to her earlobe down her throat, tugged her sweater over her head, discarded her bra, and found her peaked nipples with his flicking tongue and his hungry mouth. Thrills sparked to the core of her. His jeans slid to the floor with her skirt. He caught hold of her silken panties, tugged them to midthigh, then fingered her wettest, hottest spot, and she cried out at the climax that exploded through her.

The next thing she knew, she was on her back on the bed with Ice straddling her, putting on a condom. She had no idea where he'd found it. Nor did she care. She always carried a couple in her purse, just in case, but she had no idea at the moment where her purse was. Her mind had disconnected, as though waving her a fond good-bye as she boarded the love boat to Fantasy Island. For surely this was pure, naughty fantasy.

Ice grinned that body-melting smile, his demon gaze mesmerizing as he entered her. The friction of his thick, hard flesh against her sensitive, intimate lips brought another shocking, wonderful climactic thrill. And then they were moving together, every plunge more wild than the one before it, every coming together more delightful than the last. He kissed her and cried her name, his body going rigid with release, and she reached the crest a second later, shuddering with pleasure.

They lay side by side, her heart slowly returning to a normal rhythm, her breathing leveling to something that didn't make her feel like she'd been running through the park after the boys. It was only then that she realized she still had her boots on. It would have been funny, if she and Ice were longtime lovers, but she didn't even know this man. And considering what just went down, he might have suffered serious damage with the steel toe guards. She was usually a little more ladylike in bed. But then she usually planned on sleeping with a guy before she did it. This had just happened. And it shouldn't have, even if it had seemed predestined. Inevitable. She hoped they were both over it now. Had gotten it out of their systems. That there would be no more longing looks or innuendoes.

She slipped out of bed, taking the sheet with her,

uncovering Ice in the process. God, he was a well-built man, in every area. She swallowed hard, fearing she might want to stick around for another session, seeing evidence that he'd like that, too. Instead, she gathered her clothes and walked to the bathroom as if she weren't embarrassed, as if she had sex with complete strangers every day of the week. Let him think what he wanted. She didn't give a damn. He wasn't staying in Kalispell. She could get through the couple of weeks that he'd be here and act like an adult, especially since she'd satisfied her curiosity about what it would be like to sleep with him.

She emerged a few minutes later zipping her skirt. He was still sprawled on the bed, the blanket now barely covering an obvious erection. She liked sex with no strings attached and instinctively knew that he did, too. But he had to understand that this was a fluke. A one-time get-it-out-of-their-systems, breaking of the sexual tension between them.

She hooked her hair behind one ear. "As far as anyone else is concerned, this didn't happen."

He looked disappointed that it wasn't going to happen again right now. "If that's the way you want it, sweetheart."

"Don't call me sweetheart."

He pulled off the blanket and tugged on his jeans, commando. "Okay, babe."

She rolled her eyes. "I'm not your sweetheart or your babe. I'm not anything to you but some woman you have to work with on your latest assignment."

"Whatever you say." He worked the buttons on his jeans.

"Good." Now where had she put her purse? She headed out into the suite, the afterglow of sexual satisfaction giving her a light, airy feeling, as though she could conquer the world with a sappy smile on her face. Having sex with Ice had not only satisfied an itch, but also satiated a need for some wild, no-holds-barred, incredible sex, the kind she used to enjoy with Donnie. It was the only thing she missed about him. But today with Ice had topped all those old memories.

She heard him padding barefoot on the carpet, smelled his aftershave, and felt his presence with an awareness she didn't want to feel. Where was her purse? Her gaze swept the room, not spotting it. Recalling Ice's kisses, she couldn't concentrate. He didn't kiss like Donnie. No, this man knew how to kiss a woman, how to draw every tremor of joy from her pliant and willing flesh. Or maybe what had made the whole experience so damned great was the sense that they were challenging each other to a sexual duel of who-can-make-the-other-more-turned-on. She had to admit that had been...fun.

If only she could bottle it and sell it at the pie shop.

The pie shop. The freezer. Andrea stiffened, the reason she'd shown up here coming back to her with the strength of a teacher bawling her out for getting sidetracked and not doing her assignment. She pivoted, and Ice nearly slammed into her. "Did you or Bobby disable the freezer at Big Sky Pie for the sake of getting some drama started for the pilot?"

He stepped back, adopting an I-don't-know-what-you're-talking-about expression. She didn't buy it. Not for one minute. The look reminded her of Lucas when he wanted her to believe he was innocent after getting caught red-handed. Ice was about to lie through his perfect, glistening white teeth.

She glared at him. "I better not find out you did or... or..." Or what? What could she threaten him with? Damn. She should have thought this through before barging in on him, ending up in his bed, and threatening him. She didn't even have a good exit line. "Or else."

"Or else?" He lifted a brow, intrigued or amused. Or both. "What will you do to me? If it's anything like what you just did, I might be tempted to deserve it."

She grew as hot as chili powder and figured she was probably the same color. She stalked to the door, found her purse there, on its side, the contents spilled. *Must have dropped it when the kissing began.* She grabbed it by the handle, shoved her ejected items back inside, and left, furious with herself and more than a little dismayed.

She could not let this happen again, could not fall for another guy who was wrong for her in every way... but one. Once was enough. She had to consider what was best for her sons. And that was not Ice Erikksen. He was as far from daddy material as Donnie had been, but she'd been too young to realize that. Older and wiser meant she couldn't go with her heart this time.

She drove around town for half an hour trying to

calm down, then headed to her mother's to pick up the boys. The two-bedroom rambler with the neat yard sat in the middle of a neighborhood of homes built long before Andrea had been born. The garages and alleyways were behind most of the homes.

She parked out front and hurried up the walk to the front door. It was locked. She used her key. "Mom, why is the front door locked..." The question died on her tongue as she walked through the living room and into the kitchen, realizing she was alone. She checked the backyard. No one. Her mother's car was gone. She'd probably run to the store. For milk. Andrea decided to have a cup of tea while she waited.

She returned to the kitchen, noticing that a milk carton sat open on the counter with two small glasses and a paper plate of cookies. One glass was full, the other had just a small amount in the bottom and splashes of milk all around it as though Mom had been startled while pouring. It wasn't like her mother to spill something and not immediately clean it up. Or leave milk sitting out. A finger of unease traced her spine. She shook it off, but to make sure, she'd just phone her mother.

She dug around in her purse for her cell phone. It wasn't there. She went out to her car to look for it. Not there either. As she was heading back in to call her mother's cell with the landline, Logan ran toward her from the neighbor's lawn, but it was the look on his face that set her heart tripping with alarm. Had something happened to her mother? "Logan, where's Gram?"

"At the hospital."

Mom! "Oh my God, what happened to her?"

There were tears in his blue eyes, and his face was chalky. "Lucas fell off the porch, and Gram thinks he broke his arm. She took him to 'mergency. She tried calling you, but you didn't answer."

"When did this happen?"

"A couple hours ago." He sobbed. "Everyone's been trying to phone you. Where were you?"

Where she'd been made her sick. She hugged Logan's shaking body to her own, stroking his dark brown hair, comforting him while guilt and self-loathing flooded her.

"Why didn't you answer your phone?" His tone accused.

"I can't find my phone. I think I left it at work." She used a tissue to wipe his tears. "Come on, buddy. Let's go see how your little brother is doing."

Once they were both safely buckled in her SUV, Logan burst into tears. "I'm sorry, Mom. I didn't mean to do it."

"No one's blaming you, Logan. It was an accident."

"He was being a chicken. He wouldn't jump so I gave him a n-nudge, b-but he went flying and l-landed on the concrete hard. I heard a crack."

Andrea shuddered, as if she'd heard the crack, too, a sound she doubted would leave her son's memory for a long time. As she drove, she recalled how worried she'd been that his recent irritation with his little brother would manifest into something ugly, but she'd never thought it would involve physical violence. More like bullying. Logan had learned a harsh lesson, but she suspected another devil was weighing on his young mind.

"I promise I won't be mean to him ever again."

"I'm glad for that, Logan, but not every accident ends the way your dad's did. I'm sure Lucas will be okay." She injected an upbeat tone into her voice, hoping to soothe Logan, and wanting to believe that Luke was okay. "He'll probably just have to wear a cast for a while. Keep a good thought. Say a prayer."

They arrived at the Kalispell Regional Medical Center's emergency entrance, and Andrea scanned the lot, finally spying her mom's Subaru wagon, the old gray mare. Relief flushed through her, and she thanked God that she hadn't missed them. She parked, and they scrambled out and into the hospital, hands gripped together.

Nerves filled Andrea's throat, and fear washed her stomach. Logan held so tightly to her hand that she knew her little boy was terrified. Her own mind kept chanting, *My baby, my baby, my baby*, shaming her for not being there to keep Lucas safe. Logically, she knew that wasn't always possible, but logic had left town the second she heard about the accident.

How serious was his injury? And how did she protect Logan from the guilt he so obviously felt? She scanned the waiting area. No Mom. No Luke. She made for the check-in desk. "Where is Lucas Lovette?"

"And you are?"

"His mother."

"Sure. Let me see." As she referred to her computer,

Andrea wanted to scream, to tear into the treatment area and hunt him down, but the woman must have realized how fearful they were. She rose and motioned. "If you'll come with me."

A moment later, Andrea heard him. "I want my mommy."

Her heart clutched. She shoved the curtain aside. "I'm here, Lucas. Right here."

He shuddered, snuffled, and she knew he wanted to crumple into her arms, but she couldn't sweep him into the bear hug they both ached for as the doctor was applying a cast to his left arm. But she kissed his cheek, snuggled him, and assured him that it would all be okay, peering over his head at the doctor for her own reassurance.

The doctor nodded, explained that it was a simple break in the forearm, and that the elbow-to-wrist fiberglass cast would immobilize the bone and promote healing. Andrea felt the tension in her chest subside, but her mother looked a bit ashen.

A ten-year breast cancer survivor, Delores Norbert understood how precious life was. She faced whatever was thrown at her with a stoic attitude, including her wild, spirited daughter and her rambunctious grandsons. She handled her own ailments with quiet bravery, but when one of her chicks was ill or in trouble, her usual calm deserted her. Andrea caught her hand and gave it a "Thank you, I love you, Mom" squeeze and got one in return.

Logan sidled over to Lucas. "That's a pretty sick cast."

"It's copper for Montana State University," the doctor said.

Both Lucas and Logan had MSU T-shirts, and he told Lucas, "Like the Grizzlies."

Lucas swiped at his damp eyes and straightened, obviously buoyed by his big brother being there. "I know."

Logan took the cue, doing a sudden turnaround from guilt-ridden to protective older sibling, as though he couldn't let anyone see how upset and scared he was, especially not Lucas. "Don't worry, gizmo, I'll help you with everything. Maybe Mom will get us a couple of silver marker pens to write on your cast."

"Will you, Mommy?" Lucas asked.

"On the way home," Andrea promised, thinking her knees might give way and wishing she had someone to lean on the way her sons had each other. A sister, a brother, a husband.

The thought rattled her. She didn't need anyone, especially not a man, but every once in a while it seemed like a great idea. Lately, it seemed like a great idea more often than once in a while. As the doctor finished up, the two boys chatted. The best medicine for Lucas right now was his big brother and vice versa.

She dragged her mother into the hallway to find out exactly what the injury was and what the doctor had told her about it. But her mother was no help. "I was too shook up to understand most of what he said. Where were you? I was so frightened. I tried phoning and phoning. When you didn't answer your cell, I tried the pie shop, but you'd gone."

"Logan told me you were trying to reach me. I'm really sorry, Mom. I must have left my phone at work."

Her mother raised an eyebrow and crooked one hip. "Don't lie to me, Andrea. Some man answered your phone. He said his name was Ace."

"Not Ace." Andrea blanched. What exactly had he told her mother? "It's Ice."

"Ice? Like in ice cubes?"

"Yes."

"God, don't tell me you're running around with a rap singer."

"No. He's not—"

"Whatever." Delores waved a dismissive hand that said she didn't need to know. "You're old enough to run your own life, darling, but I just hope you know what you're doing and not getting involved with another Donnie Lovette."

# Chapter Six

Ice stood at the apartment door debating whether or not to knock, uncertain what awaited him on the other side. He might be walking right into the fist of an irate husband or lover. He didn't need that. Hell, coming here was a bad idea. He spun on his heel, retreating back toward the elevator, the heels of his biker boots heavy on the creaky floorboards. As he jammed his hand into his pocket, his fingers struck a solid object. He glanced back at her apartment, damning himself a coward. He had to give the phone to her no matter what. If he got a punch in the face, maybe it would knock some sense into him, kill this persistent desire that one roll in the sack hadn't squelched.

Who was he kidding? He wasn't here out of any nicety to return her phone. His little head was steering this shipwreck.

*Rule 1: No fraternizing with the cast.*

He released a self-deprecating laugh. He hadn't just fraternized...he'd started something much more dangerous. Something he'd never felt for a no-strings-attached piece of ass, something he didn't understand and couldn't explain to himself.

He raised his hand to knock on the door, and her mother's words rushed into his head. "Tell her Lucas broke his arm."

*Who the hell is Lucas?* He couldn't very well ask Andrea's mother, so he hadn't, but the question had plagued him for hours. What bothered him most, though, was why he gave a shit.

His fist connected with the door, harder than he'd meant it to. He heard movement on the other side and stepped back, just in case. Someone peered through the peephole. The door inched open, a chain in place. Her blond hair, damp as though from a shower, fell to her shoulders. Her face was scrubbed of all makeup. Blood rushed straight to his dick, and he bit back a groan, knowing he was in some kind of trouble that he'd never been in before.

Her big brown eyes were guarded. "What are you doing here?"

Her hushed tone made him suspect she didn't want whoever was home to hear. Lucas?

"I—" His throat was so dry that he choked on the word. He didn't intrude on another guy's territory. Not ever. Well, not knowingly. "May I come in?"

"No." She closed the door enough to unhook the chain,

then slipped out into the hallway, shutting the door softly behind her. His heart began a hard, unsteady thud, and he didn't know why. Andrea wore a long T-shirt—which showed she clearly wore no bra—her long legs enticing him, her feet stuffed into tattered, fuzzy blue slippers.

Her stance radiated cold, but fire burned in her gorgeous eyes. "How did you find out where I live?"

"Your address," he lied, thinking on his feet obviously not his best asset, "is in the paperwork you filled out for your interview."

She should have seen through the lie, but he had the impression she just wanted him gone. "What do you want?"

If she'd look down, she could detect that herself, but her gaze was pinning his. He held out her phone. "I thought you might need this back."

"I do." She snatched it from his hand and held it in a death grip. She seemed to want to ask him something, but instead she said, "Thank you." She turned to go back inside.

He didn't want her to leave yet. He wanted to pull her into his arms and run his fingers through her damp hair, taste again that incredible mouth. "About this afternoon..."

Guilt spread across her face, and his worst fears were confirmed when she said, "It shouldn't have happened."

His stomach dipped. She was involved with another guy. Shit. He had no business sticking around, making her feel worse than she apparently already did about their tryst. "Guess I'll see you tomorrow."

"No, I won't be working for a couple of days. Lucas needs taking care of."

And there it was. All he needed to know about her. For some reason it pissed him off. "Look, maybe cheating on your husband, boyfriend, whoever this Lucas is, is okay with you, but I don't tread on other guys' territory. Not knowingly. So next time you have an itch that needs scratched, don't come knocking on my hotel room door."

Andrea's mouth had dropped open, but no words came out even though she seemed about to light into him. Something held her back, some secret he saw in her eyes. Her words were clipped. "Don't worry. That's one mistake I won't repeat."

He returned to his hotel suite, cursing himself for thinking even for a minute that the reason he'd felt something for Andrea was that she wasn't the man-eater every woman he'd ever cared about turned out to be. Bobby was finishing up the dailies. "You look like hell. Wanna grab a beer?"

"No," he barked and slammed into his room, the room that now reminded him of her at every glance. He stormed back into the living room. "Yes, I want someplace noisy where I can get shit-faced. Let's go."

\* \* \*

Ice thought Lucas was her boyfriend or husband or something? If that weren't so infuriating, she'd laugh. Where did he get off anyway? Her mother's warning rolled through her mind like a neon ticker tape. "I hope you know what you're doing and are not getting involved with another Donnie Lovette."

They weren't involved. They wouldn't be involved. She wanted nothing more to do with Ice Erikksen. Going there. Sleeping with him. It had been like a compulsion, like someone else had been in charge of her. She hadn't the will to resist him, didn't want to resist him. She hadn't wanted anyone that much since...Donnie.

God, maybe Molly was right. Maybe it was just that she missed having a fella of her own. Maybe it was time she started dating with an eye toward someone to build a future with. If she didn't look for men in bars, the dating pool might yield some decent types who weren't out only for a party. She could ask some of her friends for suggestions. Even if the thought of blind dates made her cringe, she had to start somewhere. Right?

"Mom, are you going to get dressed and pick up the pizza?" Logan asked, his blue eyes radiating impatience.

"We're all starving," her mother said, glancing up from the book she was reading Lucas. "Don't know why you refused to have it delivered."

"When you taste Moose's pizza, Mom, you'll know why."

"It's good, Grammy," Lucas said. "Don't forget Aunt Molly's pie, too."

"Don't worry. I won't." She was just relieved that Lucas had an appetite and was okay with her leaving for a little while. Andrea headed for her bedroom, quickly brushed her hair, and dressed in jeans, high-heeled cowgirl boots, and a zipped hoodie. A little mascara and lip gloss and she grabbed her purse. "Back in half an hour at the most with pizza, pie, and maybe even some ice cream. Disney movie is in the DVD player, Mom. Logan can get it started."

As Andrea drove across town, her mind kept going back to Ice. The strange longing in his compelling blue eyes touched something deep in the core of her very being. It felt as though she were in unfamiliar territory. But she wasn't. She'd slept with men before and instantly regretted it, and yet somehow this was different. She didn't regret it as much as she wanted to do it again. What was the matter with her? So what if he made her body sing? That wasn't the only thing a woman needed. She groaned. Was she destined to only ever fall for Mr. "Hot, Sexy, but No Commitment" guys? The possibility brought on an aching sadness.

She parked near the pie shop, then hurried through the cool autumn night across Front Street, beelining for the rustic-looking building with the old-time, swinging saloon doors. A sign proclaimed MOOSE'S WORLD FAMOUS PIZZA. According to legend, politicians, blue-collar workers, and corporate leaders used to call this their place to meet and socialize. Even Evel Knievel claimed to have come up with his Snake Canyon jump one night in this bar.

The interior resembled something that might have been around in the Old West days with battered barn siding, wooden tabletops, and walls that customers had carved their names or sayings on. Peanut shells littered the floor. The place had an energy that wrapped you up like the hug of a good friend. The bar took center stage in the middle of the room, amid wooden booths and picnic table seating. The noise level was a dull roar punctuated by the occasional cheers or moans depending on how the Thursday night NFL Vikings game, which was showing on several big screens, progressed.

Andrea made straight for the bar, but her order wasn't ready yet. She ordered a glass of Malbec and moved to an end bar stool, squeezing in between a couple of men, not glancing at either of them and not realizing how tense she felt until the wine began to ease the knots from her shoulders. It had been a hell of a day. And it wasn't over yet. She wasn't the world's worst mother. Was she?

"Andrea, what brings you here on a school night?" asked the man on her left.

Startled from her thoughts, she gazed over and up into a familiar, friendly face. Wade Reynolds, one of Quint McCoy's best friends, a bottle of Bud Light in hand, smiled down at her. It spoke to how preoccupied she was that she'd missed noticing the six-foot-four widower. If she had to run into anyone, she was relieved that it was Wade. "Only another parent would think seven p.m. on a Thursday night was late."

He grinned, a slow curling of his mouth, and she realized he was extremely handsome in a quiet, unassuming way. He was raising his preteen daughter on his own since cancer took his wife four years earlier.

Andrea knew, if anyone understood the vagaries of single parenthood, he did. She told him about Lucas.

"Only Moose's pizza and some of Molly's pie à la mode will do tonight."

"I'm sorry to hear that he broke his arm. Poor little guy," he said, his sympathy cutting straight to her heart. "I'm hoping Moose's pizza will have a similar effect on Emily. She's having trouble adjusting to the move into town."

"I heard you were selling the cherry ranch," she said. "I take it the sale went through?"

"Yep. Last month. I bought a three-bedroom craftsman. It needs some updating, but it was move-in ready for our purposes now."

"Sorry the cherry farm didn't work out for you."

"Ah, that's okay. It was Sarah's dream, not mine. I'm glad to be back to construction. I was all thumbs as a farmer. The guy that bought the orchard though seems to know his stuff. I think Molly will be glad of that next cherry season."

"Speaking of cherries…" She told him about the fiasco with the freezer.

He nodded. "Quint asked me to take a look at the wall in the cold room. Seems like the liquid might have done some damage to the drywall. Doesn't sound extensive, but it's the kind of damage that can eventually cause mold."

Drywall damage. Another expense that the pie shop didn't need. If she discovered Ice Berg Productions had anything to do with that, she'd make them pay for the repairs. As she thought that, she felt a strange tingling down her spine, the sensation of being stared at.

She glanced around the bar, thinking maybe her name had been called, that her pizza was ready, but it wasn't that. And then her bad-boy antennae twitched, and she knew.

She spied him, directly across the bar. His partner Bobby and a bunch of women were crammed into a big booth, cheering on the Vikings' opponents, the Seahawks. Was that BiBi beside Bobby? It was. *Interesting.* But not interesting enough to divert her attention from Ice's penetrating blue eyes. His gaze unnerved her. She couldn't read him, but he didn't look away from her, not even when a lusty redhead sidled up and draped an arm over his shoulder. He ignored the redhead, shrugging her off, and kept staring at Andrea, and Andrea couldn't pull her gaze free of his.

What the hell did he want with her?

"Your pizzas, Wade, Andrea," the waitress said, stepping right in front of Andrea and eclipsing her view of Ice.

Andrea jerked as though she'd been shaken, coming back to herself. "Oh, great. Thank you." She paid for her two small pizzas, then turned to Wade as he also stood. "Gotta run. It was nice talking to you."

"Yeah, maybe I'll see you at the pie shop?"

"That would be nice." She touched his hand, just a friendly gesture, hoping Ice would notice, and not understanding why she gave a hoot if he did. She took a step back and felt her feet slipping out from under her. She saw Ice react, reach for her even from across the bar, an impossible save, and yet arms did lift her. Wade.

"Whoa." He pulled her to her feet and into him, laughing. "Gotta watch out. Those peanut shells are slippery."

Andrea hated how hot her face felt, how clumsy and flustered and unlike herself she'd become since Ice Erikksen came into her life. Wade grabbed hold of her pizza boxes and his own, insisting on walking her to her car. She gave him a grateful smile and fell into step beside him. As she reached the swinging doors, she felt that prickling on her neck again, knew without glancing back that Ice was watching her leave with Wade. She moved closer to the tall man, as though he were more than her friend. The hell with Ice Erikksen. Why should he care who she dated? And why wouldn't he quit staring at her as if she'd done something wrong?

\* \* \*

Andrea yawned as she made her way through the house, checking to be sure the doors were locked, turning out the lights in the living room and kitchen. The boys each had their own room, a luxury that eased the stress of two opposite personalities trying to share the same space. Walking into Logan's space felt like entering a war zone; more clothes occupied the floor than his closet. Lucas, on the other hand, couldn't stand chaos. His room had everything in its place. Often she'd catch him absently picking up and putting away Logan's things if he was in there chatting or playing with his brother.

But peeking into Lucas's room now, she paused,

thinking she was so tired she'd accidentally gone into Logan's room. A mound of blankets and a pillow occupied the floor next to Lucas's bed. The night-light showed that Lucas was sound asleep, his arm propped on his favorite stuffed teddy bear. As she crept closer, she realized that the heap of blankets was Logan, also asleep. Her heart squeezed. *Big brother keeping his promise to watch over little brother.* Tears sprang to her eyes. Poor little guys. They'd had a tough life lesson today, but they shared a bond as strong as steel.

She was sure that Logan would be stiff from sleeping on the floor all night, but she left him there, knowing he'd be better emotionally for it.

She climbed into her own bed exhausted, hoping Lucas would sleep the night through, wishing she could absorb his pain instead of feeling helpless and hurting for him. She fell asleep thinking there should be something more a mother could do than offer gentle touches, soft reassurances, and distractions for her hurting child.

Sometime later, she began to dream of one sexy bad boy who knew exactly where to kiss her, who could raise her passion to levels she'd never experienced before, who was wrong for her in every possible way. A man she still wanted with every ounce of her being. Damn. She was doomed. She woke up shaking, in a cold sweat. It was still dark. She'd been asleep for only two hours.

She got up and went to check on the boys again, trying to shake off the dream, but it wouldn't leave her. As she went into the kitchen, Andrea spied Molly's caramel apple pie, cut herself a slice, heated it in the microwave, and lifted a forkful to her mouth. The crust flaked against her tongue, and the sweet apple and spices dissolved like honey, the taste sensation as delightful a pleasure as great sex. As she continued eating, every bite had her mind tumbling, trying to make sense of her life. Molly was right. She did miss having a permanent man around, someone to share the everyday events, someone to hold her when unwanted dreams woke her in the night.

As she scooped up the last morsel of pie, she had an epiphany. She was making bad choices, acting with her heart instead of her head. In an ideal world, the choice of her heart would be what was best for her entire family, but that wasn't how things always worked. She needed to face it. Ice was a carnal fling. A last hoorah. He wasn't staying in Montana. He had a life in California. His job took him across the country from one coast to the other. She was a small-town Montana girl who hadn't a wanderlust bone in her whole body. None. It might sound a bit Dorothyish of her, but to Andrea, there was no place like home. Montana was in her blood, in her bones, in her heritage. Why would she ever want a man who didn't feel the same?

She had to break those old, bad-for-her patterns. She wasn't pursuing anything in her life. She was just surviving, just taking care of the boys and working to fulfill that duty, but there was no goal for something better. Where did she see herself five years from now? Or ten? Alone? Did she intend to always manage a pie shop? Was that all she wanted out of life?

No. No. Getting the job in the real estate office had been a fluke, but that was where she'd discovered that she liked running a business. Maybe someday she'd like to run her own business. Whatever that might be, she didn't know at this moment, but the idea was appealing. First, though, she wanted to secure a daddy for her sons. And tomorrow, she was going to make a plan.

*The find-a-stepdaddy plan.*

# Chapter Seven

Anxiety swirled through Andrea after she dropped the boys at school and headed for Big Sky Pie. She'd assured Lucas's teacher that she'd have her cell phone on at all times if, for any reason, the school might need to call. Logan, of all people, told her not to worry, that he would keep an eye on his brother. Her heart ached that he was taking on the man-of-the-house role. He was a kid. His childhood shouldn't be filled with grown-up responsibility, but she would allow him that duty for one more day. She hugged him and told him how proud she was of him.

She headed to work, not looking forward to facing Ice today, but to her relief, the Ice Berg Productions van was nowhere in sight. She parked a block away from the pie shop, enjoying the short walk through the mild, sunny morning that held a hint of autumn chill. Fall was her favorite season, but she'd been so self-absorbed the past couple of weeks that she hadn't even noticed the leaves turning red and gold. Until now. Those glorious hues against the blue of the sky reminded her of some priceless oil painting locked behind museum walls, available only for those lucky folks within visiting range. But this was nature's watercolor—real, tactile, and free for anyone who cared to notice. A smile stole across her face. She didn't need to be rich or travel the world to find happiness or wealth. She could just look around. It was everywhere, and it was free.

Andrea entered the pie shop through the back door, feeling bolstered. A blast of pure sugary delight met her nose. It was like walking into a Halloween carnival where vendors hawked caramel apples and pumpkin tarts.

"Andrea!" Jane, BiBi, and Molly sang out in unison.

The welcome chased away the last of her nerves, and that cold tight ball in her chest warmed. She smiled. If she should decide to leave the pie shop at some point for employment elsewhere, she would dearly miss this aromatic, affable environment. "Good morning, ladies. Looks like you've had a productive day already, and it's not even nine thirty."

"We have," Molly assured her. "How are you, dear?"

"I could use some coffee. Can I get some for anyone else?"

Molly arched an eyebrow, a look that said, *You're avoiding my question*, but she didn't press the matter. "I'd like some, thank you. Decaf, please."

"Me too," BiBi said, peeling apples at the work sink by the row of windows, sunlight kissing her short hair. A piece of green apple peel stuck to her elbow. "But I want mine double jolt."

"No coffee or tea, not even decaf. Doctor's orders, until after this little one is born. And not even then if I decide to breast-feed—" Jane broke off, going bright pink. She licked her lips self-consciously. "How is Lucas?"

"He's better. Back to school with Logan as his personal bodyguard in case anyone gives him flack." Andrea tucked her hair behind her ear, her earlier anxiety leaking back and into her voice. She filled them all in on the past two days, on how Lucas would make a full recovery, and they shared their respective feelings of relief.

Molly made a cooing sound. "Those boys are so precious. I remember when Quint was little…" And she went off on a story about Quint and her late husband, Jimmy, going fishing and returning home to her sweet cherry pie.

"I broke my arm when I was a kid," BiBi said, interrupting Molly's story and earning herself a frown of displeasure. BiBi didn't seem to catch that. She twisted toward Andrea, waving the peeler as she spoke. "It will heal fine. I can still remember, though, how that darned plaster cast itched."

"I hear the new fiberglass ones aren't nearly as uncomfortable," Jane said, poking bits of caramel candy into the apple mix, and then braiding strips of dough over the top.

"And," BiBi added, "you can get them in the sickest colors."

"How are those apples coming?" Molly asked BiBi with a hint of annoyance.

It wasn't like Molly to verbally snipe at anyone, and Andrea frowned. She suspected her boss was cranky about more than the assistant chef's interruption. The stress of the economic loss of the fruit, the possible damage it could do to Big Sky Pie's reputation, and dealing with insurance agents was more likely getting to her.

"Just about done," BiBi said, giving the apples a last wash to remove any clinging peels.

Andrea left to get the requested coffee as well as her own. When she returned to the kitchen, BiBi was standing beside Molly, paring apples. BiBi said to Molly, "You were right, you know."

"Of course I was…about what, dear?" Molly had her back to the work counter, putting a couple of pies into the ovens.

Bibi laughed. "I've been doing some unofficial apple pie taste-testing at various restaurants around town, and each and every time, the pies they serve are like eating half-cooked apple chunks. Al dente is great for veggies, or noodles, but not for fruit desserts. It's like the chefs yank the pies from the oven too soon. Just like you said."

"Well, how about that?" Molly smiled at Jane. "Some of what we've been teaching our assistant is getting through."

Molly didn't seem to notice BiBi stiffen, but it wasn't lost on Andrea, and she jumped in to soothe the assistant pastry chef's ruffled feathers. "Great observation, BiBi. That's why our apple pies melt in your mouth."

"Exactly," Jane said, seemingly oblivious to the tension that hung in the kitchen. She finished crimping the edges of a lattice crust, brushed the top with an egg wash, and sprinkled a bit of cinnamon and sugar over it. *Tinkerbell spreading her special fairy dust.* It was another part of what made Big Sky Pie's desserts taste so incredible.

Molly said, "We'll make some turnovers with the apples you're slicing now, BiBi."

"Sweet." BiBi no longer seemed to be feeling sweet, though, and a stilted quiet fell over the kitchen.

Andrea removed herself from the silent friction, retreating to the café to ready it for opening. Although she didn't bake any of the treats sold in this shop, she felt as much a part of Big Sky Pie as those who did. She wanted every customer drawn here for the delightful desserts to be wowed by how clean and inviting the café was.

A cleaning crew came once a week for a thorough go-through, but Andrea started her mornings putting on clean tablecloths, making sure the seating and the floor were crumb-free, the display cases smudge-free. Satisfied with her handiwork, she readied the cash register, then refilled the napkin holders and the coffee condiments.

Molly came into the café, taking a short break. It

was one of her eight-hour days, and weariness showed around her eyes, usually so bright, but at half-watt right now. "The plasterboard behind the freezer needs to be replaced."

"I know." Andrea stuck the bulk box of sweetener packets back into the supply cabinet behind the sales counter. "I ran into Wade the other night, and he mentioned he'd be checking it out for Quint."

"He was here yesterday." Molly refilled her coffee mug and sank onto the bench seat of the end booth. "It's going to cost more than the deductible, but it needs to be done to prevent mold."

Andrea refilled her mug and sat across from her. "I was afraid of that, but maybe we can make it up on the insurance for the produce."

Molly screwed up her face. "That…that Charlie Mercer. I'd like to skin his hide. He's coming over to haul that, that piece of junk to his shop and try to figure out why the motor cut out. The insurance agent insists."

Andrea wasn't surprised. "The agent has to justify our claim to the adjuster or underwriter, who has the final say before they'll cut you a check."

"I know. I'm just impatient." Molly sipped her coffee, then set her cup down with a look as though something completely different had just occurred to her. "I just had a thought. Remember when we were talking about a fella for you last week or so?"

"Yes." Andrea might have decided to instigate the find-a-stepdaddy plan, but she hadn't had any time to think about prospective candidates. If Molly had some suggestions, maybe she needed to hear them. "I remember..."

"Well, I don't think you could find a much better-looking one than that Wade Reynolds. Can't understand why some woman hasn't latched on to him by now. He's been alone for such a long time."

Wade? Andrea had never thought of him as anything more than, well, than Quint's friend. "He isn't really alone. He has Emily."

"A preteen daughter? It's not the same, dear."

Andrea took a swallow of coffee. "I think Wade is still in love with Sarah. Not sure he'll ever get over her."

"That doesn't mean he should be lonely the rest of his life."

The same could be said for Molly. Andrea shrugged, rolling the idea of Wade as something other than a friend of a friend through her mind. The notion was so far off the wall...and yet... "I don't think he's interested in dating."

*Especially not in dating me.*

"He's just extremely shy."

More than shy. He'd always sent out a "taken" vibe, and she'd respected that as only a woman can whose husband forgets his wedding vows before the ink dries on the marriage license. When it came down to it, though, Wade wasn't her type. Not a bad-boy bone in his body. Safe was how she'd describe Wade, safe and steady. Reliable. A great father. A great stepfather perhaps? Definitely. Possibly.

But he didn't turn her on.

And Ice turned her on too much. Lord, what would Molly think if she knew about her and Ice? The thought pinched already taut muscles. Wanting to placate her boss, Andrea said, "If I decide to look for someone with a mind toward my future, then I'll seriously consider Wade, okay?"

"Good. You could do worse. A lot worse."

The words burned through Andrea's conscience. She had already done worse. Ice. An image of him naked, the blanket barely covering his most impressive assets, flooded her mind, sending tremors of want through her. Damn. Having sex with him should have ended her curiosity. Her attraction. So why did she feel so drawn to him still, as though there was so much more that she had to discover?

That she couldn't let go dredged up a bad feeling. She hadn't been able to let go of Donnie either, even though he'd betrayed her again and again. She'd stayed with him until he'd dumped her like so much rubbish. The old shame reared its ugly head, taunting her current self-esteem. She stared it down. She'd recovered. Fully.

As much as she might still be intrigued with Ice, sleeping with him was a mistake she would not repeat. Finishing her coffee, she caught the time. "Yikes. I should have had the door open five minutes ago."

She scooted out of the booth, gave the display case one last glance, making sure the shelves were filled with a fresh array of pies, tarts, and cobblers, then started the CD player. The soft strumming of an acoustic guitar floated from the speakers. She hurried to the windows. As the louvers parted, sunlight swept into the café, filling the space with the final ingredient needed for that warm ambience.

Andrea worked the last window blind to find the most compelling blue eyes she'd ever seen peering in at her. She gasped and stumbled back a couple of steps, her heart tumbling in her chest like a washing machine on tilt. A curse word her daddy taught her flew out of her mouth and burned even her ears.

"What is it?" Molly asked, sounding as though Andrea had discovered a mouse running wild in the pie shop. Nope. Just one big rat.

Andrea glared at Ice, drawing a slight curl of his sexy lips, not a real smile, more like a private one that said they shared a secret. She went cold inside—hot and cold. "The film company is finally here."

"That means Zoe can't be far behind," Molly moaned. She refilled her coffee. "Before the craziness starts…have you been in touch with Dean and Betty Gardener about our blueberry disaster?"

"Not yet." Andrea pursed her lips. Giving and receiving bad news had freaked her out for as long as she could recall, though now that she thought about it, maybe it hadn't been farther back, really, than the day of her mother's breast cancer diagnosis. She was sixteen. That was the day she realized life could stop right in the middle of whatever plans or goals you'd been making. She'd watched her mother suffer through chemo and radiation, watched her father's health suffer as her mother grew sicker. She'd decided then to grab the brass ring with both fists, to live her own life fast and hard, to appreciate every day.

*Best-laid plans...*

She shirked off the trip down *unpleasant* memory lane. "I hate giving people bad news, but—"

Ice walked in. The interruption annoyed her as much as his staring in the window had. Her words dried on her tongue. Just being in his vicinity scrambled her brains into hot mush while shivers of awareness danced a happy salsa. Why did he have to smell so darned much like sex on a stick? Walk with that panther gait? Look like nothing ever fazed him? The odd thought skipped across her mind like a ghost, barely there, but somehow distracting. Important? Was he solid ice inside? Or was that I-don't-give-a-shit attitude a carefully formulated façade? Body armor to keep the world from seeing him for the man he really was?

She forced herself to concentrate on the information she needed to give her boss. "As much as I'd like to have that meeting over with and settled in our favor, Dean and Betty are still out of town at some floral shindig. They're supposed to be home tomorrow. I plan to speak to them in person. I don't want to break this news over the phone or in an e-mail. Tell me you have a backup plan that I can offer them."

"I do. We can go over that before I head home."

Relief loosened the grip it had on Andrea's chest. "Good. I'll do my best to keep from losing this gig, Molly. I promise."

"I know you will, dear." Molly gave her a big smile and patted her shoulder.

"Hey," Ice butted in, "I want to go with Andrea when she meets with the Gardeners. I want to get their permission to include their story in the pilot footage."

"What?" Molly's brows lifted toward her spiky red hair, puzzlement in her widened eyes. "Why?"

Bobby came in with Flynn on his heels, catching just enough of the conversation to add, "It'll give the pilot that 'ahhh' appeal. America will feel bad for the newlyweds. They can't get enough of that sentimental crap."

"Sentimental crap?" A flash of anger flared in Andrea at these offensive words. She gaped at Bobby, her disgust curling her hands into fists. These clueless oafs. She'd never felt more like punching someone. She'd give them a tongue-lashing if it would penetrate their alligator hides, but she'd dealt with too many rednecks not to know that these Hollywood cowboys were just as dense.

Tempering her voice, she said, "Gentlemen, this is their wedding reception."

"Yeah." Flynn spoke up for the first time, setting his hefty camera onto a nearby table. One she had just set. "Who can't relate to wedding plans going awry?"

She felt as if steam hissed from her ears. "You guys don't seem to appreciate what a wedding and reception mean to a bride. How many years she dreams of every perfect detail falling into place. How upsetting it can be when even one aspect of those plans doesn't work out."

Ice raised his hand like a kid in class waiting to be

called on. A glimmer of understanding filled his eyes. Andrea didn't say anything, just gave him a look that he should enlighten them all as to his newfound insight. In response, he said, "What Bobby meant is that this kind of life situation is something people can relate to. It has universal appeal."

Ice didn't seem to realize that, even phrased more nicely, the request itself was as tacky and insensitive as it got. Maybe it spoke to his true nature. Maybe the only thing he was hiding under that uncaring attitude was crudeness.

*Welcome to reality TV.*

Suddenly the thought of dating a decent guy like Wade held surprising appeal, while spending another minute with Ice didn't.

# Chapter Eight

～

Is this that TV thing that Quint and Nick told me about?" Wade Reynolds asked, glancing around the cold room like a big dog looking for a hole in a fence.

"We've been keeping that our secret, Wade," Molly said, "and it would be best if that continued."

Andrea agreed. Once locals figured out they could get on TV by dining or shopping at Big Sky Pie, she figured business would either come to a complete halt or boost sales to new highs. She prayed that if, and when, this happened, the ensuing result would be the latter.

"I don't want, er"—Wade cleared his throat—"I'm not comfortable with"—he cleared his throat again—"I'd rather not—"

"I think Quint would appreciate it if you'd do this

for me," Molly said in a voice as sweet as her frozen cherry pie.

*Oh, brother.* Andrea offered him a pitying smile. Molly had pulled out the big guns. Wade didn't have a chance. There was no way this nice guy could reject her irresistible cajoling. He was toast.

"Okay. I guess." He stretched his neck like a man dreading an impending noose. Andrea bit back a smile, her gaze raking absently over his loose-fitting, long-sleeved T-shirt, which displayed a defined upper body, while faded jeans cupped every intriguing masculine angle, dip, and curve beneath a low-slung tool belt.

*Damn. You might not be my type, Mr. Reynolds, but you are serious man-candy.*

Molly thanked him, then added, "I'll send you home with a fresh caramel apple pie today when you leave. Oh dear, is that the timer I hear?"

She hurried away, leaving Andrea and Wade alone. He shook his head as if to ask, *What did I just agree to?* There was an innocence about him that was charming, and something else vibrating beneath the surface like a revved motor that begged a heavy foot on the gas pedal. She'd always kind of blown him off, never looked beyond the surface. Maybe she should look.

"I think that woman could talk a drunk into quitting cold turkey," he said, lifting his baseball cap and replacing it.

"It's the pie," Andrea said. "She knows the way to a man's stomach."

A smile warmed his handsome face and stirred

an urge to bring on that smile more often. He didn't smile much, she realized. Life had given him some hard knocks, given them some things in common. She suddenly wondered if he'd like to go out for coffee sometime or a drink. Maybe a pizza. Before she could suggest it, though, Ice came into the cold room.

"The handyman will also need to sign a release." Ice extended a hand to Wade, introduced himself, and asked, "Mr. . . ."

Wade didn't seem to notice Ice's offer of a handshake, a frown furrowing his brow. "A release form?"

Ice dropped his hand and stepped back. "In case we use whatever footage you're in for the pilot. It's a standard industry form. If you're okay with that, then you can go ahead and get to work on the wall."

Andrea could see the only thing Wade wanted to "get" was out of the promise he'd just made to Molly. But again, she knew he wouldn't. He was a man of his word.

"Wade is not a handyman, Ice," Andrea said. "He's a building contractor. The only reason he's doing this, and not having one of his crew do it, is as a favor to the McCoys." In other words, show him some respect.

Ice's gaze locked with hers, another dangerous game of dare, the energy between them like a live wire. She felt herself getting turned on. No. No, no, no. She did not want anything more to do with Ice. As long as this pilot was being shot, it had to remain strictly business.

Flynn bounded into the room, camera hugged to his side, Zoe and her makeup satchel right behind him. Ice pointed to Wade. "Zoe, this is your latest victim. Do your magic."

Wade's eyes widened, but Andrea wasn't sure if it was at being called a victim or at Zoe advancing toward him with her makeup kit.

"Makeup?" he protested. "No way, José. Either we do this without that or I'll fix this wall after all of you are tucked into bed for the night."

"But you'll look like a ghost on camera, Mr. Reynolds," Zoe whined, her rainbow tresses bobbing with dismay.

"Don't care." Wade stood his ground, and he was too tall for Zoe to reach his face with her blusher wand.

Zoe glanced toward Ice, seeking intervention.

Ice shook his head. "Whatever. His choice."

Zoe looked crestfallen. But Andrea would swear Ice was more interested in the interaction between Wade and her than in what kind of player Wade would be in his production.

"Would you like me to leave, or stay?" Andrea asked. Ice's expression said what he'd like was to have his way with her, the smoldering fire in his intense blue eyes stirring inappropriate yearnings, but she'd be damned if she would blink first. "Stay? Go? Which one, oh, great director?"

A slight smile touched his sexy mouth. "Stay. Interact with him like you would any service person."

"I'm not an actor," Wade said, stating the obvious.

"Neither am I," Andrea reminded him. "Don't fret about the camera. Just ignore everything in your peripheral vision and do what you'd do as if no one were here but you . . . and me."

"I need to do Andrea's hair and makeup first," Zoe said.

Andrea groaned silently. She hated the heavy makeup and oversprayed hair-dos, but having seen some of the video dailies with and without those, she understood the necessity.

"She looks pretty good already," Ice said. "Just be quick about it, Zoe. I want to get this shot done."

*Pretty good?* The backhanded compliment smarted. She glared through her lashes, her gaze raking over his chinos and polo shirt. Some designer brand, no doubt. Her clothes might only be top-of-the-line Walmart, but she thought she rocked today. Hot pink sweater and skinny jeans tucked into her white Durangos with the tiny blue hearts and silver grommets. Okay, the boots were designer. The only thing she splurged on, but only if they were on sale.

She followed Zoe to the ladies' room, encouraging her to hurry, too. "And don't go heavy-handed on me today, okay?"

"Do I ever?" Zoe gave a toss of her rainbow-hued head, causing a row of fake eyelashes to dislodge and land on her fuchsia-blushed cheek.

Andrea plucked the faux eyelashes between her finger and thumb and handed them to Zoe. "Less is more."

"God, I so don't agree with that. If given the choice, always choose more."

Andrea did a silent eye roll, earning her a frown from Zoe. A few powder puffs and comb teases later, she stood near Wade in the area of the damaged wall.

The light on the camera on Flynn's shoulder shone green, and Ice had set up klieg lights to expose the repair sight. The heat from the intense carbon bulbs had already raised the temperature in the cold room. Molly would not like that. They had to get this segment over and done with in the first run-through.

Ice slammed the clapper. "Action."

Wade jumped, then laughed at himself and wiped his palms on his jeans. "This is like real Hollywood-y. I didn't expect that."

"Okay," Ice said.

Andrea was surprised Ice hadn't told Wade that the pilot wasn't some home movie, but as "real Hollywood" as it got.

"Again from the top," Ice said. "Action." *Clap!*

Wade took a deep breath as though getting a hold on his nerves. He hunkered down on his haunches.

The bright lights meant for filming actually helped to visually delineate the moist plasterboard, Andrea saw. "What do you do first?"

"I'm checking the perimeters to ascertain the outer-most edges of the dampness." He patted his hand above and around the center of the damage. He pulled a tool from his belt.

"What's that?"

"Retractable utility knife."

"Looks like a box cutter."

"Same thing," he said, touching the wall again and scoring the plasterboard as he went. "I'm marking the damaged area and a wider band above the dampness."

Andrea was vaguely aware of Flynn moving about for better angles, Ice overseeing the whole scene. She watched Wade work, fascinated and curious about the process. Her former experience in real estate hadn't included going out to new builds or viewing houses under construction. She ran the office.

Wade said, "Next step is cutting out this section that needs to be replaced."

Andrea nodded absently, her mind still on the past. Although she'd toyed with the idea of obtaining her real estate license a couple of times, she realized that the crazy hours the job required of Quint would be required of her, too. That gave her pause. Yes, when the market was up, she could've made more money than she earned running the office, but potential buyers expected realtors to be available weekends and evenings. To manage that, she'd have had to move in with her mother. She shuddered. She loved her mother to pieces, but she equally loved her independence, and besides, her mother would worry 24/7 if she and the boys lived in her house. They'd all go nuts.

Wade grunted, pulling off the piece of wallboard, then he reached into the cavity and explained, "Checking to see if the framing is wet."

She held her breath. "How bad is it?"

"Not as bad as I thought originally." He pulled free of the hole and wiped his hand on a work cloth he pulled from his back pocket. "Quint will be happy. I won't have to charge him as much as I'd estimated."

"Finally, some good news." Andrea heard the exaggerated relief in her voice and knew that this dialogue would end up cut and pasted for a dramatic sound bite, a teaser for promo purposes. Use a bit of dialogue that sounded like dire news, but when you heard the whole sentence, it was actually a positive, not negative, result. Viewers watched for the negative.

"In fact, the damage is pretty minimal." Wade looked up at her, rising as he spoke. "It helps that the floor is concrete and that the liquid was contained for the most part. Just need to replace this damp, ruined drywall here."

"Great, then you should have it done today."

He shook his head, retracted the blade of the utility knife, and returned it to his tool belt. "I can't replace the wallboard yet."

"Oh?"

"In order to assure that there won't be any molding to deal with down the road, the space needs to be completely dry before I can replasterboard it. I'll set up a portable heater for the next couple of days."

"A heater?" An image of the fresh fruit going the way of the frozen filled her mind, knotting her stomach. "This is a cold room. We can't have the room heating up." The klieg lights were already warming the air too much.

Wade bent over and grabbed the chunk of plasterboard he'd cut from the wall, extended his lithe body to his full six-plus, and offered her that rare grin. "Don't worry. I'll direct the heat to this one spot and set the temperature to the minimum."

Andrea felt herself smiling back, reacting to this very good-looking man.

"Cut," Ice called. "Thanks, Wade. Looked good to me. If you'll go with Bobby there, you can sign the release form."

"I need to set up the heater first. It's in my pickup," Wade said, then ambled out with Bobby.

Flynn lowered the camera and unplugged the kliegs. "Flynn, follow that Wade guy and get some shots of him with his truck."

"Huh? Oh, okay." Flynn hurried to catch up with Wade.

The bum's rush, Andrea thought, delivered by the demon manipulator. She'd intended to walk with Wade to his truck and bring up the possibility of meeting up sometime for a drink. Damned Ice. She spun on her heel with every intention of chewing him out, but froze under the gaze of those mesmerizing eyes that haunted her dreams. His grin said he had her where he wanted her—all to himself.

He needed to be set straight on a few points, first that she wouldn't be manipulated. Maybe he couldn't help himself, being a director, but she didn't like it. She closed the gap between them as though she were glad to be alone with him. She got up close and personal, in full-on flirt mode, fingering his collar, feeling the pulse at his neck quicken, hearing his intake of breath. She leaned into him as if she meant to kiss him and whispered, "If you'd wanted to get me alone, sweetheart, all you had to do was ask."

He started to reach for her, but she pulled back. He cocked his head, studied her, something bothering him, but not what she expected. "How's Lucas?"

The question seemed to come out of the blue, like an angry hornet biting into her exposed flesh. Why had he asked about her son? What did Lucas have to do with him? Nothing, that's what. "He's none of your concern."

Ice pressed his lips together, nodding. "You're right. He's not. I was just...being polite."

She nodded, knowing she needed to draw a line with him. "The other day with you was an awful mistake. It can't happen again. Ever."

"Awful?" A soft laugh vibrated in his throat. "I don't believe you...and you know as well as I do that it will happen again..." He was staring at her mouth, and then her breasts—which were standing at attention, either from the cold of the room or the heat of his gaze. She should leave now, but her brain wasn't paying attention. It was listening to the baser requests being made by the glances of this so-wrong-for-her man.

"I don't have any expectations," she said. "I don't want anything more. No strings."

"What if I want strings?"

"You don't want strings." She couldn't help chuckling at the absurdity of that. "Any woman harboring that fantasy only has to sleep with you to realize it's a foolhardy notion."

His eyes clouded, a sure sign that she'd dented his ego. "What does that mean?"

Oh, God, why had she opened this can of worms? How did she explain that she'd had a man exactly like him? That she knew from experience he was only in it for himself. He didn't want her for her. He was only turned on by her loving wild sex as much as he did. What could she say that would make him stop coming after her for more? "Don't get me wrong. I enjoy hot, dirty sex as much as anyone, especially with a lover who knows his way around the female body. But like most women, I want something more."

"Such as?" The glint in his eye said, *Bring it on.* He was up for any challenge she wanted to throw at him. Literally up for it, she realized, judging by the bulge in his chinos.

Her resolve wobbled, her grasp on the situation slipping through her fingers. But she couldn't think when he looked at her like this, when she wanted to feel his mouth on hers, his arms around her, his body pressed close.

He came toward her. "Can't think of anything?"

"Yes. I can." But nothing was coming to her. Nothing she'd say to him.

He'd backed her into a corner, heat issuing off him, making her panties wet and her heart thunder. She felt like a moth fluttering toward a killing light. If she wasn't careful, she might let him strip her naked right here, just to extinguish the flame that burned for him. So much for being in control of any area of her life. She was a screwed-up mess.

He groaned her name, shoved his hands into her hair, and captured her mouth in a brain-tingling explosion of lust. She wanted to claw his clothes off and climb on top of him, right here, right now in the pie shop. He broke off the kiss, panting, his forehead to hers. "What is it about you..."

Andrea couldn't catch her breath, couldn't answer, despite realizing the question was rhetorical. A clatter sounded in the hallway. *Oh, my God, Wade was back.* They jumped apart and moved several feet away from each other, Ice readjusting his pants, she straightening her sweater and licking her kiss-swollen lips. Flynn came in first, but the male voice behind him was not Wade's. And she could hear Molly, too.

"It's the freezer guy," Flynn said, clueing them in as he swung the camera to his shoulder and aimed it toward the doorway.

Charlie Mercer and a noisy hand truck appeared a moment later, with Molly following, squawking like an irate mama bird berating a predator who'd tried to rob her nest. The fact was that Charlie had sort of robbed the nest by selling her a faulty freezer. If the cause of its death was natural. She caught a silent exchange between Ice and Flynn that roused her suspicions all over again.

Charlie nodded to the others as he spotted them.

"I'm here for the freezer," he announced, apparently not realizing everyone knew that already. Andrea stood to one side, gathering her composure, measuring this ebullient man with a thatch of salt-and-pepper hair, a matching mustache, and the most honest face Andrea had ever seen. Was that face his perfect conman's tool? The reason people bought his sales pitches? Or was he what he seemed?

He moved the hand truck to the upright freezer. "Molly, I swear to you I had no idea this would happen. I can't tell you how sorry I am."

"Humph. *You're* sorry?" Sarcasm and sorrow twisted through her words. "I've lost my winter pies if I can't find that fruit elsewhere. That's a huge loss for a new business, Charlie Mercer."

"Damn. I hadn't considered that, Molly." He looked so genuinely upset and sympathetic that Andrea wondered if he actually was. "In deference to my friendship with Jimmy, I tell you what I'll do. I'll pay for half your losses. Will that help?"

Molly looked as though she was about to tell him what Jimmy really thought of him and that he should pay for all of her loss, but Andrea could see his offer was slowly sinking in. Half was better than nothing, and the insurance might cover the rest. Molly lifted her chin, her expression softening as she gazed up at him. In that moment, Andrea realized Charlie had a thing for Molly, and Molly knew it. Maybe he always had. Maybe that was why Jimmy trash-talked Charlie to his wife. "Why, Charlie, that's a very nice offer, and I'm going to accept."

Andrea could almost hear Molly thinking, *But only because you sold me a bill of goods and deserve to pay for the damage it caused.* Molly, however, was obvi-

ously smart enough to know when to keep her opinion
to herself.

Or maybe she realized the camera was on, that she
was playing to an audience, and giving them "sentimental crap" would make this pilot sell.

*   *   *

*"Don't settle for a tiny slice of the pie, son, not when
you can have the whole bloody thing."*

His father's decades-old advice scrolled through
Ice's mind like credits on a screen as he handled the old
digital camera as if it were an Oscar bestowed on him
by his peers. It had been a present on his seventh birthday, a gift from his internationally acclaimed director
father, Ivan Magnus Whittendale. At the time, Ice felt
as though he'd been given the keys to the kingdom. In a
way, he had. For this "key" released the evil genie that
turned his happy boyhood into a wasteland.

His gaze flicked around the hotel suite. He should get
moving. Bobby and Flynn were already at the pie shop,
but he'd slept in, ordered breakfast sent up, and was
lingering over a last cup of coffee. He'd needed to be
alone. To sort through the unrest this shoot was causing
him, the sentimental homesick feeling that he couldn't
even explain. Like wanting to phone his mother.

As if she'd take his call. Instead he'd reached for
this camera as a reminder of all the reasons that calling
her would be unwise. He hadn't understood his father's
advice at seven years old, but he soon understood it too
well. When the dust had settled, he'd found himself

stowed away in a private boys' school in Northern California, his name legally changed to Ian Craig Erikksen, the latter being his mother's maiden name.

They'd done it for his sake, the lawyer told him. To keep the scandal from tainting him in any way. *So that nosy reporters couldn't hunt me down and get the real story, more likely.* From his prospective, he might've been abandoned on the moon. His father blamed him for the divorce, for the loss of his "box office gold." That was what he'd called Ian's mother, a genuine movie star adored by the world, whose presence in a movie guaranteed a hit every single time. His adoring mother could no longer stand to look at Ian because, except for having her blond hair, he was the image of his father.

He didn't know any of this then. All he knew was that he'd done something bad, and it had cost him everything he cared about. Sitting in his dorm room, scribbling his new initials over and over, he'd realized they spelled "ice" and how apropos that was for how he felt inside, like a frozen block where there used to be a soft, fuzzy warmth. He never celebrated another birthday, never allowed himself to even consider getting involved with someone, friend or lover, who might demand a piece of his heart. Even Berg was expendable. As far as Ice was concerned, love was the nastiest four-letter word in the dictionary.

But here he was, feeling something he couldn't name, for a woman he didn't know.

Not that the unwanted stirrings for Andrea were

love. Hell no. But whatever they were, he couldn't seem to shake loose of them. Normally sex had the opposite effect. If he nailed a woman who'd roused his libido, the minute it was over, he could walk away without a backward glance. No regrets. No second timers. *No strings.* Andrea's words taunted him. Why couldn't he stop thinking about her, wanting her? Why had he hated the smiles she'd been exchanging with that hammer jockey?

His body grew hard just thinking about their kiss in the pie shop. Damn it.

At times like this, he wished he had someone to talk to. But this was not a conversation for his mother. He lifted his phone and went on the Internet. His parents had moved past the scandal eventually, married others, had other children. Children they seemed to love. Ice had met none of them. He wasn't included in family holidays or get-togethers. His choice as much as theirs. If ever he felt like catching up on his parents or stepsiblings, he only had to visit an online celebrity gossip site. None of their names jumped out at him today.

But something else did. A featured story. Dread and ire swirled in his gut as he read:

What son of celebrities is currently in a small-town, northern redneck state engaged in filming a reality show in a pie shop, of all things? Hint one: daddy owns iMagnus studios. Hint two: mommy is movie star royalty.

# Chapter Nine

❧

You could take a trip with those bags under your eyes," Zoe told Andrea the next morning. "Some concealer should do the trick. Whenever your eyes look this puffy, though, try some cucumber slices."

*Or I could try not to have erotic dreams about a certain director.* Andrea yawned. "Didn't sleep well last night."

Zoe daubed cover-up under Andrea's eyes; brandished her mascara wand, blush brush, and lipstick; then stepped back to gauge her handiwork. "That's better. Dark circles gone."

Andrea went into the ladies' room to check that Zoe hadn't gone overboard. She removed a bit of the eyeliner and tamed her hair to something that resembled her usual style. Ice Berg Productions would have hidden cameras in the café today to catch exchanges with the staff and customers. Apparently they needed some everyday activity to supplement the scripted materials. And if any of the customers proved interesting, they would contact them for a possible recurring role in future episodes should the pilot actually sell.

Bobby and Flynn were just securing the hidden microphone at the counter. Molly would not allow any at tables or in booths. No one wanted to be sued for invading someone's privacy. Andrea set about her morning routine, switching on the music, starting the coffee and espresso, putting clean tablecloths on each table, filling the condiment holders, checking the cash register, and finally looking over the display case. Brand-new fruit pies, cream pies, and a variety of tarts and cobblers filled the shelves. The air was scented with the perfume of fresh-baked apples and caramel.

Andrea had decorated the coffee counter with a tiny pumpkin, a witch, and a fake spider to commemorate Halloween.

"Place looks great," Molly said.

"Yep." Now if some customers would show up. "Oh, hey, I have a surprise for you."

Molly winced as if in pain. "I've had enough surprises lately, thank you very much."

"This is a great one."

That brought an immediate twinkle into Molly's bright blue eyes. She wiped her hands on her apron and gave an encouraging nod. "Well, I like the sound of that. Did you book a date with Wade?"

"No." Andrea laughed, then remembered the hidden cameras and hoped they weren't already rolling. She didn't want her dating life on tape. "My mom treated the boys and me to dinner last night at that new diner across town. I noticed their dessert menu was sorely lacking. The waitress overheard Mom say they should carry some of your pies and mentioned that to the manager. Long story short, they want to offer Big Sky Pie desserts in their diner."

Instead of a smile, Molly reacted as though Andrea had struck her, stepping back and frowning. "But won't we lose customers who would come to this café for dessert by offering our pies elsewhere?"

"Well..." Andrea couldn't swear that wouldn't happen. "We might at first, but in the long run, it will put our brand out there and give folks more reason to come here when they aren't eating at that diner."

Molly pursed her lips, thinking it over, then nodded. "I guess that makes sense. Okay, then. I'll leave the pricing up to you and Quint. Just remember we need to make a profit, too."

Andrea never forgot the bottom line. "In regard to that, we won't be delivering the pies, they will come here and pick them up. That saves us the cost of fuel and a delivery person. And they aren't going to 'special order' anything to begin with either. They've agreed to make their selection from whatever we're already producing on any given week or month."

The last of the frown between Molly's brows eased away, and she was nodding her head, smiling. "The more I think about this, the more I like it. If it works out, we might be able to expand on it down the road. Good job, Andrea. Oh, they will use some sort of signage or mention on their menu of Big Sky Pie, right?"

"I have Callee doing placards like she makes for our display case."

"Sounds like you've got everything under control. Let's get this place open. We have pies to sell."

Bobby and Flynn had settled into the middle booth, heads together over an iPad and coffee. Andrea left them to it, taking care of her own chores. She raised the blinds, unlocked the door, and found two cars parked in the lot. The customers exited their cars at the same time.

"'Bout time you opened up this morning, Andrea."

She wasn't sure which one had said it, but she offered a cheery smile, genuinely glad to see them. "It's the same time as always."

She welcomed them inside and took their order, bringing them coffee and cobblers. Another customer arrived. A stranger. A lean brunette in her early thirties, Andrea estimated, wearing black slacks and a tank top with a black cardigan. Large glasses perched on a hawkish nose. She took a seat in a corner near the window, balancing on the edge of the chair like she might dart off at any given moment. *How curious.* She set a laptop on the table, and Andrea guessed she might be a writer. She ordered coffee and a lemon tart.

A half hour later, Sharla Tucker, the chamber of commerce's director of special events, came in. A big woman unafraid of bold color, loud jewelry, or big hair, she gave Andrea a warm greeting. "We're surprising the mayor today for his birthday, and that man does love Molly McCoy's pies. What would you recommend?"

"Well, this month's specialty is the Granny Smith caramel apple pie, but we also have a spicy pumpkin rum pie."

"Ohhh. That's sounds naughty, but yummy." Sharla's finely painted brows twitched, and a smutty smile spread across her face. She perused the display case and its delightful selection of desserts. "Hmm. Which would the mayor like best? You know what? I'm going to take your suggestions and get both the apple and the pumpkin rum just to be on the safe side."

As Sharla left with two Big Sky Pie boxes, Andrea began to hum quietly to herself, her mood lifting. She'd just closed the cash register when a familiar voice said, "Hey, Andrea. Long time no see."

It took her a second to realize the man standing across from her was Dave Vernon, aka Dave the Realtor. She barely recognized him. He must have lost thirty pounds and gained a lot of muscle. Even his dark brown hair looked different, longer, yet more stylish than his preferred crew cut.

"Well, hi, Dave. I think the last time I saw you was when you closed the deal on Callee and Quint's house." While she worked for Quint, she'd speak to or see Dave at least every week or so. He was a hardworking realtor, nose-to-the-grindstone kind of guy with a quirky sense of humor. "You're looking very fit."

The compliment seemed to make him ill at ease. He shifted on his feet and glanced around, tugging at his tie like a guy wanting to ask a woman a serious, perhaps embarrassing, question. She couldn't even guess what he wanted. "Would you like some pie or coffee? Or both?"

The question seemed to make him more uncomfortable. He toyed with the ring on his right hand, a realtor's ring, she knew. "Coffee, I guess."

"Have you tried Molly's pies?"

He sighed, regret heavy on his face. "Can't. Sugar diabetes. I don't suppose Molly makes any sugar-free pies?"

Andrea shook her head, but the suggestion wasn't lost on her. This was another way to expand the pie shop's business. "Not at this time, but I think she has plans for that."

The lie wasn't meant to hurt, but to keep, a potential customer. It was a great idea. She would mention it to Molly and let her and her chefs take it from there.

Dave accepted the coffee from her, remaining at the counter while she refilled the other customers' cups. When she got back and started a fresh pot of coffee, Dave said, "I heard a rumor."

"A rumor?" Andrea straightened and stared at him, waiting for him to expand. When that didn't happen, she said, "About?"

"Oh, I don't know. Maybe I shouldn't have mentioned it." He worked at the knot in his tie again.

"There's no pretending you didn't already mention it, Dave. So out with it. What rumor?"

His face got a little pink. "It seems like a fool thing now that I'm here and can see no such thing is going on."

A weird fluttering started in Andrea's stomach. Was there some sort of rumor going around town about the pie shop? Like rats in the cold room? Bugs in the food? Drugs or something? Small town. Smaller mind-set sometimes. Everyone keying in on gossip and spreading falsehoods across the county. Was that the reason sales had fallen off? She dragged Dave over to the end booth and made him sit, aware that the cameras might see them, but that whatever rumor was out there wouldn't be recorded. "You'd better tell me what this rumor is right now, Dave Vernon."

The shock of being dragged to the booth kept him quiet for a minute more, then he lowered his voice to a whisper. "I heard there's a reality show being filmed in this pie shop. I laughed it off, but my source insisted it was true, said it's even on the Internet."

"What?" Holy cow. Andrea let the impact of that sink in and wondered if it accounted for this morning's sudden rush of customers. As she thought about it now, she realized that everyone who'd come in seemed to be smiling too much, fussing with their clothes, their hair . . . as though they might be on camera at some point.

She groaned inwardly.

"It isn't true, is it?"

Andrea sighed. If she confirmed it to Dave, the news would spread like wildfire. They didn't want that. She rolled her eyes as though the very idea were ludicrous. "What do you think?"

"Yeah, that's what I thought." He grinned and drank his coffee. "You know, that apple pie smells so darned good, I wish I could eat it, but since I can't, I still think I'd like to take one back to the office for my staff. Then they'll know for sure that I checked out the rumor with the source." He handed her a ten-dollar bill.

She boxed the pie and brought it and his change to the booth, sitting with Dave for a few more minutes.

Dave asked her about her boys and offered her sympathy over Lucas's broken arm. "I don't suppose you'd like to have a drink some night, if I gave you a call?"

She quirked her head, pleasure and wonder skipping through her. Wasn't Dave full of surprises today? She hadn't ever considered him dating material, but then, like Wade Reynolds, he'd never set off her bad-boy meter. She found she didn't hate the idea of meeting him for a drink and gave him her number. "Call me, and we'll work something out that suits both our schedules."

As she watched Dave walk out, she felt her bad-boy antennae start to vibrate. But it wasn't Dave. This was coming from behind her. Ice. Had he seen her handing Dave the slip of paper with her phone number on it? Overheard her accept a tentative date? She hoped so. Maybe that would discourage his advances and the desire for him that haunted her waking hours and her sleeping ones.

This town was full of a lot of nice guys that, until now, she'd never considered getting to know better. But she intended to start. She couldn't go on the way she was—always getting caught up with a guy who didn't make her feel good about herself except for that space of time when they were having sex.

Ice moved up behind her. "We have a problem."

If he was talking about her dating life, which was none of his business, then that was an understatement. She spun around to find him closer than she'd calculated. His gaze was like a slate blue storm cloud, and intense anger wafted off him in waves.

"That steam billowing from your nostrils better not be rage directed at me."

"Someone leaked to the press about the reality show."

"I just heard, but it wasn't me."

"Didn't think it was."

"The site that originated the news is located in Hollywood. I'm pretty sure the leak is in my own crew."

The glare he cast at Bobby and Flynn gave her a chill. It didn't bode well for an ongoing partnership. "Do you really think either of them would betray you that way?"

The conflict in his eyes said he didn't know for sure, but she knew that his believing it even for a second had already damaged friendship and partnership. She advised, "If I were you, I wouldn't accuse anyone, just ask nicely if they're aware of it. Don't make accusations you can't prove. What if you're wrong?"

He blinked. She'd penetrated his ire, but he was still too furious to calm down. "Go outside, walk off the mad, then speak to Bobby."

The brunette in the corner rose, shoving at her glasses and heading straight for them. Her laptop was still on the table. Andrea assumed she wanted more coffee or another tart. She started toward the woman, but the woman wasn't interested in her. She wanted to speak to Ice. "Aren't you Ian Craig Whittendale?"

Ice paled beneath his tan, a stunned expression spreading over his handsome face.

Andrea froze, gaping at Ice, at the woman, and back at Ice. Had this woman been waiting for Ice to come in? Was this connected with the Internet leak, or about something else? Had she called him Whittendale? But Ice didn't answer the woman. He turned and headed into the kitchen. The woman tried to follow, but Andrea cut her off. "I'm sorry. Everything from here back is employees only."

"Like he's an employee. Not. Son of the rich and famous, that's who he is. He can run, but he can't hide. I will find him."

Andrea plastered on a smile. "Can I get you something else?"

"Sure, I'll take another one of those tarts."

Andrea wished the woman would take a hike, but kicking out paying customers wasn't taking care of the bottom line. She wanted to hunt Ice down herself at that moment to find out who this woman was and why she'd called him Ian Whittendale. What was that all about? She brought the brunette the coffee and another tart, pumpkin this time.

She wanted answers and realized, instead of Ice

providing them, perhaps she could ask this woman. "So what brings you to our little town, if you don't mind my curiosity?"

"I'm a reporter for CEN, Celebrity Entertainment News in Los Angeles." She passed a card to Andrea. Rita Grace.

"And you think Mr. Erikksen is a celebrity?"

"Honey, I don't know what line he's fed you, but he is the real deal. The firstborn son of Ilse Craig and Magnus Whittendale. I'm writing an unofficial biography about his family, and he's my missing link. He knows all about the scandal that broke his parents up when he was a kid. I only need a few minutes of his time. Do you think you could arrange that?"

"I'd have better luck arranging an interview with the man in the moon." The news that Ice was the son of such famous people zinged through her brain like a shorted wire. "Knowing Ice, you just had your few minutes."

The glasses got another shove as the brunette's eyebrows bumped. "I'm not that easily dissuaded. What do you know about him?"

Too much and too little, Andrea realized. And yet, on some level, she felt as if she'd always known him. But she didn't. Not really. That scary feeling filled her stomach. She'd been duped, sucked in by her own shortcomings, her fatal flaw laughing its ass off at her gullibility. Ice came from Hollywood royalty. Her subconscious needed to get over him. He was a trust-fund baby; she was a blue-collar nobody. Opposite ends of the social spectrum. He'd grown up privileged beyond anything she could even imagine. The reporter was still waiting for a response, but Andrea wasn't about to say anything to upset Ice more.

He already thought his partner had betrayed him. Maybe he even suspected Bobby of inviting this reporter here. He'd seemed hurt, yet so angry that it was as if he was embracing his rage to avoid some secret pain. It made Andrea all the more curious about his childhood. What had happened to him as a kid? She decided she'd like Ice to tell her that—if he would—rather than hear it from Rita Grace.

When she realized Ice wasn't going to show his face in the café again, Rita left with a promise to return. Then Andrea went in search of Ice. She found him in the kitchen, seated at the work counter holding a meeting with Jane, BiBi, Molly, Callee, and Quint. Bobby and Flynn were noticeably absent. Ice told the staff what he'd told her. "Cat's out of the bag. Someone posted on the Internet that I'm filming a reality show at Big Sky Pie."

"Oh, no." Jane's hand went to her mouth, and her cheeks grew pink. "Why would someone do that to you?"

Good question, Andrea thought. Did that Celebrity Entertainment News site pay for stories like that? Or was someone trying to harm Ice Berg Productions? Or Ice?

His forehead furrowed, and his shoulders seemed to carry a heavy burden. "I'm sorry to say that there are more people in my business who'd rather stab you in the back than shake your hand, Jane."

"It's true. That's how my dad lost his TV show," BiBi said, apparently forgetting her father's role in the downfall of his own career.

Andrea and Molly exchanged a glance. BiBi's father, Chopper Henderson, was a renowned chef with a line of cookbooks, his own cookware, and a show on the Food Network. He was the Howard Stern of the cooking industry, his blunt opinions winning him many critics and millions of fans, until he made gay slurs about one of his fellow FN coworkers. And his fans became instant haters. The scandal hit every media outlet in the world, and within days, he'd lost his show and his sponsors, but not his big ego or bulging coffers. He'd retreated to his massive, secluded log home on nearby Flat Head Lake to lick his wounds and set impossible standards for the daughter who worshiped at his feet.

"Exactly what does this mean for all of us?" Callee asked, her chestnut curls bobbing as she spoke.

"Yeah," Quint said, concern etching his handsome features as he reached for his mother's hand. "Mama's got enough to deal with just running this shop. She doesn't need any added stress."

"Quint darling, don't you fret about me." Molly cast an adoring glance at her son. "My cardiologist assures me that my heart and I are both strong as horses. Besides, I figured this would happen at some point. We can't hide everything we're doing for the pilot from our customers. Sooner or later, someone was bound to get curious about that Ice Berg Productions van always parked outside or about Flynn and his camera. Well, it's happened sooner is all. That's the way the crust flakes sometimes."

Andrea saw Ice watching the interaction between mother and son with conflicting emotions flitting through his eyes: a trace of wonderment, a touch of envy, and a ton of sorrow. *Weren't he and his mother close?*

He cleared his throat. "Here's what you should be on guard about. You're probably going to be bombarded with questions from curious family, neighbors, friends, even strangers. It's up to you to be evasive. Don't engage in a conversation with them about the pilot. Tell them that you've signed a confidentiality agreement and can't speak to them about it. Period."

"Not even to my husband?" Jane asked, guilt written on her face.

"As our marketing director, your husband already knows about it, Jane," Quint reminded her.

She blushed. "Yeah, well, I don't tell him everything."

Everyone chuckled.

Ice said, "But he understands the process. He might be able to give you some tips on how to handle people, if you feel you need them. But remember, the rest of you still cannot discuss the reality show with anyone except each other."

"Why not?" BiBi asked. "My dad—"

"No. Not your dad. If any of the things we have already filmed leak or competitors got wind of it, they could beat us to the market, and you can kiss this show good-bye. Is that what you want?"

Everyone shook their heads. Andrea found that even she didn't want the production to shut down, and the realization gave her a rush, like acting on something she knew was wrong, but doing it anyway. But she feared her wanting the show to continue had more to do with not wanting Ice to leave.

"You didn't have any of us sign a confidentiality agreement," BiBi pointed out, looking as though she thought Ice was an idiot.

He looked as though he felt the same. "I let that slide, but I shouldn't have. My attorneys are all over my, er, me about getting it done immediately."

"Closing the barn door after the cows have escaped," Molly muttered.

"Yep." Ice nodded sheepishly, then implored of each of them, "I'd like to take everyone's word that you won't leak anything in future, but I need to get that in writing. I'm not saying any of you leaked this. I'm sure that came from my end. Nor does this mean that I don't trust any of you. But I need this or I'll have to walk away. I can't risk losing everything I intend to invest in this project if everyone isn't on board. And it needs to be settled. Right now. That's why I asked Quint and Callee to be here."

"I'm willing to sign it," Quint said. He shoved his hand through his blue-black hair, glancing at the staff. "If any of you, however, has a problem with it, it's okay. We just need to know."

"I'll sign it, too," Jane said.

"Yes, me too," Andrea said.

With everyone agreeing, Ice passed out the documents and pens. "Ms. McCoy, I apologize again for this fiasco."

"If life was a well-oiled machine, Ice, it would be too dull to endure." Molly signed her paper. "A good dustup once in a while adds some spice."

Ice smiled. He gathered the papers, thanking them all. As the meeting broke up, he came directly to Andrea, catching her elbow, moving her to a corner near the back door, and speaking so that only she could hear. "Is *she* still in the café?"

"Rita? No. That doesn't mean she isn't lurking somewhere outside."

He nodded, his face growing thoughtful, his mind probably calculating how to avoid the persistent reporter.

Aware of everyone else in the kitchen, she kept her voice low. "Is Ilse Craig really your mother?"

His head snapped back as if she'd slapped him, and his lip curled in disgust. "She gave birth to me, if that's what you're asking."

For half a second, he reminded her of Lucas, vulnerable, his emotions laid raw, a wound in his eyes too deep to reach. Her heart hurt for him. She wanted to pull him to her as she would her son and reassure him that all would be well. But Ice wasn't a little boy. He was pure, grown-up male, every dangerous, sexy inch of him. He shook himself like a big dog shaking off rain, seemed to recover control of his emotions and tuck them back into the box from which he'd allowed them to momentarily escape. He was, she realized, a proud man, a private man, and even though he would deny it, a man with demons.

As curious as she was about those demons, she knew he wouldn't open up. Not to her. He held his secrets close. Maybe awful secrets. She didn't need to befriend someone who could bring elements into her sons' lives that were not good for them. Whatever his deal was, it wasn't her problem.

She needed to remember that and not feel sorry for him like she'd done with Donnie.

Andrea went back into the café, delighted to see that more customers had come in. At this point, she didn't care why they were showing up to buy pies; she was just glad they were. She had to refill the display case three times in the next two hours. The surplus of pies was dwindling, and that was a good thing.

Molly went home exhausted, but smiling.

Suzilynn arrived and took over at the café counter, giving Andrea a chance to sit down for a cup of coffee and some girl chat with Callee, who'd returned with the placards for the diner.

"They look great," Andrea told her. "You've really found your niche."

"And I thought I wanted to be a chef, when all the while my passion lay in creative design. I really am enjoying myself as never before." Callee glowed, her happiness a tangible thing. It hadn't always been that way, and Andrea was glad for her. But she also seemed to have something on her mind. Was she worried about the Internet thing? Or something else?

Andrea sipped her coffee as Callee leaned across the table. "So, that director is hot. Did you notice the way he looks at you? Like he'd like to eat you for dessert."

Andrea's face flared with heat. She couldn't admit to Callee that he already had and that she kept longing for a repeat.

"So are you going to let him?"

Coffee spurted from Andrea's mouth. Callee reared back, laughing, and rescued the placards. "Don't try to tell me you haven't thought about it."

Andrea winced, suspecting she probably looked as guilty as if she'd just robbed the pie shop. "He is way out of my league. Did you know he's Ilse Craig's son?"

Callee gasped. "The movie star?"

"That's the one."

"Well, talk about hidden depths."

"And not exactly the kind of guy looking for a single mom with two little boys." Or any other kind of permanent relationship.

"Hah, he'd be lucky to put his Dan Posts under your bed for life."

"You mean his surfboard." They laughed and drank more coffee.

"Then how about we find you someone who would love a sexy, blond single mom?" Callee said, pulling her phone from her purse and glancing absently at the screen as though expecting to see a text or e-mail. "There are a lot of great-looking guys in this town. Lovely, lonely men."

"Funny you should say that." Andrea tucked her hair behind her ear and told her about Dave the Realtor asking her out to coffee, and that she was also toying with the idea of getting to know Wade Reynolds better.

"Good. Do it."

"Which one?"

"Both, of course. Don't limit your options until you find out if either is worth pursuing past a drink or two." Callee glanced at her phone again.

"Is something wrong? You seem...distracted."

Callee sighed and shoved the phone to the side. "I'm sorry. It's not me. It's my best friend, Roxy."

"The one who married the Seattle Seahawk?"

"The one who's divorcing the Seattle Seahawk."

"The one who owns the waterfront bistro on Puget Sound?"

"Yes. But things are not great in paradise. Washington is a fifty-fifty state. That means when you divorce, you split everything down the middle. She and Ty agreed that he would take a larger share of the sale of their house and then release his interest in the bistro. Turns out, though, that his new fiancée wants to be a restaurant owner and doesn't see why they can't retain joint ownership of the bistro. Roxy would rather slice and dice the sweet thing and serve her for an entrée. She's miserable. I'm going to Seattle for a few days to help her figure things out."

Andrea smiled. "Roxy is lucky to have such a great friend."

"She'd do the same for me. Did do the same, actually." Callee smiled. "Quint isn't too happy to have me gone, even though I won't be away for more than a week. But it is the first time we'll have been apart since we called off the divorce."

"Tell him to use that time to go fishing with his buddies."

They burst into laughter again. Fishing had almost caused Callee's and Quint's divorce, but in the end, Callee had discovered fishing was something she and her husband enjoyed doing together.

"Give Roxy my best wishes. Divorce sucks." Especially if you'd married a cheater.

Callee touched her hand and gave it a squeeze. "Love is not for weaklings, but if you find the right guy, it's worth giving your whole heart to him. I found that out the hard way. I hope you'll have what Quint and I have one day, Andrea. You and those darling sons of yours deserve it."

Andrea realized she would love to have what Callee had, but she didn't think it was written in the stars for her. Not unless she could break her habit of falling for bad boys. Starting with Ice Erikksen.

# Chapter Ten

*Ice crossed the lobby of the hotel on his way to the parking lot, his focus on the front door, his mind on Andrea and all the things he wanted to do to her. With her. *Meet me in the parking lot*, her text had read. Maybe he could drag her back to his room. A smile played along the edges of his mouth, anticipation speeding up his steps.

"Ice." A woman's voice stopped him in his tracks. He spun, expecting to find Andrea. Instead, it was Rita Grace. *Shit*. He scowled and turned back toward the lobby exit, kicking up his step another notch.

"Ice, how do you feel about your mother filing for divorce from her latest husband?"

She hurled the question like a stone. It was meant to shock him into giving a reaction. A sound bite. Something she could record and blast over the Internet. Her

mistake. His mother had been divorced too many times
for the end of her latest marriage to bother him. He
didn't even miss a step. There had only been one of his
mother's divorces that hurt him. The first one. And that
one was his fault.

Buried memories bobbed to the surface like cof-
fins in a flooded cemetery, and a haunting guilt washed
over him. He lifted his chin, squared his shoulders, and
kept moving, convinced that nothing bad could catch
up with him as long as he didn't stop. The reporter's
heels clicked on the tile floor behind him. He began to
whistle, drowning out the sound.

The automatic door whooshed open. He strode into
the cool morning air, welcoming the crisp feel on his
hot face, the fresh, fresh air into his lungs. Nothing
smelled as good as Montana on an autumn morning.
No smog or pollution. Just pure oxygen that even the
stench of an aggressive paparazzo couldn't foul.

"Ian, what do you think of the rumors that your
mother is sleeping with her newest director?" the
reporter shouted as she hurried after him, using his
given name to personalize her attack, a weapon to hook
his attention and cut him deeper.

His frantic gaze swept the parking lot. Where the
hell was Andrea? And then he spotted an older SUV
with the passenger door wide open, a sexy blonde
behind the wheel. He ran for it, jumped in, slammed
his door, and snapped the seat belt. "Go. Now. That
reporter is after me."

Andrea did as asked, pulling out of the parking lot

with a squeal of tires and merging recklessly into traffic with a blast of horns and near collisions. The reporter skidded to a halt, looking frustrated, but staring at her phone. *Fuck.* She'd probably taken photos of him running away and driving off in this SUV. It would probably be up on the Internet within minutes.

But he was too keyed up to consider possible consequences. He held on for dear life as Andrea wove in and out of lanes and suddenly cut into the drive-through at Starbucks and hit the brakes. He jerked toward the windshield, then flopped back against the seat. "Where the hell did you learn to drive? Nascar?"

"The farm." She didn't expand.

He slanted toward her. "Is that some place Montana teenagers go to learn to drive?"

The warmth of her musical laugh made him smile. "It's where I grew up. A ten-acre farm on the outskirts of town. Dad had a couple of cows, a couple horses, chickens, you know. Old MacDonald. I was driving the tractor when I was eleven."

"I hope none of the animals were harmed."

"Nothing but a few rows of corn." She inched the car forward, grinning.

God, she had a beautiful profile with a perfect straight nose and pouty lips. His libido jumped, and he wondered if he could coax her to exit this drive-through and find somewhere to park. He wanted her in his arms, but then he inhaled. Chanel. The scent reeled his mind to the past, to the worst moments of his life, moments mirrored in this recent news about his mother, yet another private family event he'd learned from the god-damned media. His gaze went to the side mirror. Were they being followed?

As though reading his mind, Andrea asked, "What did Rita Grace want this time?"

He rubbed his jaw. "To tell me that Ilse Craig is divorcing her latest husband."

"Oh. I'm sorry." Her voice was full of commiseration.

He shrugged, but didn't look at her. "It comes with the territory."

"I meant about your mother's divorce."

"So did I." He pulled sunglasses from his jacket and put them on, as much to thwart the glare of the sun as to hide his eyes. "Marriage is a joke. It's impossible to be faithful."

"Maybe in Hollywood..."

He stared at her profile again and found his breath catching. "Don't tell me you believe in commitment and loving one man 'til death do you part?"

Andrea pushed her hair behind one ear, revealing a gold hoop, a soft, kissable lobe, and a sweet expanse of creamy neck. God, how he wanted to take her to bed again.

She sighed loudly. "I've seen that kind of love."

A cynical laugh spilled from him. "Yeah, in the movies or in books, but not in real life."

She flinched. Had he struck a nerve? She hadn't said she'd "had" that kind of love, or even that she'd "known" that kind of love, only that she'd "seen" it. That was the kind of statement someone made when love had disappointed them, when hope of finding the "real" thing still thrived. But none of that told him what he really wanted to know. Who was Lucas? Why did she keep skirting that question? Obviously he was someone special.

Andrea inched the SUV ahead to the speaker, placed her order, then reeled off his favorite, surprising him. She'd remembered what he'd asked her for the first day they met. He added, "Make it a venti."

"Did I forget that? Sorry. Make them both venti," she said into the speaker.

Ice gave her the cash to pay for their drinks, their hands bumping, awkward, exciting. The disturbed shift of her lovely brown eyes told him she'd felt it, too. She might swear that she would never make love with him again, but he could tell she wanted to. As much as he did.

She pulled up to the window, conversing with the barista while they waited for their drinks. He couldn't shut off his mind. If Lucas was her lover, boyfriend, or husband, then why had she fallen into *his* bed with such abandon? Especially since she believed in long-term commitments. She was a puzzle that he ached to solve.

She wore no adornments, no rings or bracelets or watch. He frowned. Now that he thought about it, he couldn't recall seeing her wear any kind of jewelry, except for earrings. Maybe she had a metal allergy. Maybe that was why she didn't wear a ring? Hell, he was sick of wondering and speculating. "Are *you* in a committed relationship?"

She glanced sharply at him—the only visible sign

that he'd surprised her, but turned her gaze away, staring at the car in front of them. She said, "Would it bother you if I were?"

What kind of question was that? Images of their hot afternoon romp slammed into his mind. Of course it would bother him—if he were the guy she was supposed to be committed to. "Nope. None of my business."

"Then why'd you ask?"

The better question was: Why did he care, if she didn't? He swallowed hard. Damn it, why? Why did just looking at her have his pulse revving, his blood thundering through his veins? She dressed more modestly than women he was used to, just a peek of leg showing from between the hem of her navy blue skirt and the top of those sexy, calf-high boots. And yet it was somehow more alluring than if she'd been wearing do-me pumps and a miniskirt.

He shook his head at the absurdity of it. He lived in Malibu. Any day of the week, a steady stream of females wearing bikinis—which left little to the imagination—roamed the beach in front of his house. But Andrea in work clothes had him hotter than a California wildfire and in a perpetual state of lust.

He squirmed in his seat, his jeans suddenly tight in all the wrong places.

She paid for their drinks, then handed him one, their hands grazing again and his heart skipping. *Look away, think of something else. Like football. Or surfing.* But as she edged out onto the road, his gaze wandered over her curve-hugging blouse, to her skirt, and lower, settling on the boots. This wasn't the pair she'd worn the day they'd made love. Those had been tan with blue inserts. He smiled. He had the bruises to remember those boots by. These were white with tiny beige hearts. "You like boots, huh?"

She smirked. "I do. But I only buy them on sale."

She said that as if she needed to justify spending money on something she really wanted. The women he knew spoiled themselves at every whim. He'd bet Andrea's budget didn't include a "whim" column. *What would she do with an unlimited credit line—like mine?* Recalling her shabby apartment building, he knew what he'd do. Find a better place to live.

That was something he'd like to do as well. Although his Malibu home was in a gated community with a guarantee of privacy, he always felt more like he was being caged in than the press being locked out. What he wouldn't give to live somewhere like . . . like this town, where friendly folks were the norm, and paparazzi were rare.

The thought surprised him. He'd never even considered living in another state. Or in a small town. But this place was growing on him. Maybe it was the friendly, unpretentious residents. Maybe it was the changing seasons. Maybe it was the beautiful blonde beside him. Or maybe she just had him so mixed up he didn't know what he wanted.

He only knew what he didn't want: to be hounded by the press wherever he went. His gaze slid to the side-view mirror, but what was he looking for? He didn't even *know* what vehicle Rita Grace was driving, or if he could spot a car that might be following them.

Still, he turned to look out the rear window of the SUV, and that's when he saw it. A shiny red object on the backseat right behind Andrea. He reached for it. A little boy's toy car. A shock slammed through him. A child? The one thing that hadn't occurred to him about Andrea was that she might be a mother. *Lucas?*

Before he could ask, Andrea said, "Is that reporter following us?"

"I don't think so."

"I hope not. It's bad enough that she showed up at the pie shop again this morning asking what time we'd be expecting you."

A pain started in his chest like the reporter's nasty little claws digging into his flesh, filling him with dread. "Well, now that she knows where my hotel is, I doubt she'll bother with the pie shop."

"I hope you're right. But what if she won't go away? She might leak stuff to her Internet news outlet and ruin any chance the pilot has of selling."

"Exactly." He'd been worrying about that since yesterday, but was hoping not to have to deal with it just yet.

"Isn't there some way to make her go away. Legally, I mean?"

*If only.* "Freedom of speech and all that. She's not breaking any laws, just doing her job. So pretty much our hands are tied."

"But she could ruin everything for all of us."

"Reporters like her are a particular brand of ruthless. Efforts to make them go away only increase their determination to find out anything they can that is none of their business. The best thing is not to engage with her at all."

"Well, Molly won't let me evict her from the premises as long as she keeps buying pie and coffee. Molly is afraid she might write something negative about Big Sky Pie. And Rita is the reason we're going to meet with the Gardeners at their shop and not ours."

"I might have to sic Bobby on her."

"Didn't you think Bobby was the reason Rita came to Kalispell?"

"I could've been wrong about that."

"But what if you weren't? Aren't you afraid what else he might tell her?"

*Yeah. Hell. I don't know.* "I don't want to talk about her." He tugged on his seat belt, which felt like it was strangling him. "Tell me about this couple we're going to see. Why is everyone in the pie shop intent on making their reception perfect?"

"I'd rather they tell you themselves, since we're here." She pulled off the road and into the parking area of a strip mall, then drove to a space in front of The Flower Garden. "It's a true story of enduring love and overcoming amazingly difficult obstacles to end up together."

"Sounds like the kind of sentimental"—the look she gave him stopped him cold—"er, *hook* that has viewer appeal." Even though he'd tempered his words, he heard the disdain in his voice and reminded himself not to show that when he met the Gardeners.

His gaze scanned the florist's front windows, catching on the orange and black theme, interspersed with greenery and twinkle lights. "They should have named it The Pumpkin Patch."

"Huh?"

He pointed to the display window. She smiled and shook her head. "'Tis the season."

"Yeah, well, it's too cutesy for my taste." Ice undid his seat belt.

Andrea cut the engine and faced him. "I'm sure you're used to more sophisticated florist shops, but in this part of the country, we're pretty homespun."

She had a point. The shop where he had a standing account in Beverly Hills was three times this size with every exotic flower imaginable. "I was expecting something larger."

"Bigger doesn't always mean better."

"Well, yeah, but variety—"

"Isn't everything. If they don't have it in stock, they can order it."

"But what if I wanted to walk in and buy you, say, some yellow orchids?" *Like your hair.*

"Not a fan of orchids or roses or exotic flowers. I'd rather have a bouquet of spider mums."

He couldn't believe it. What woman didn't love orchids or roses? This woman apparently. That off-kilter sensation swept over him again, letting him know everything he knew about women might not apply in dealing with this one.

Andrea switched the subject as handily as she released her seat belt. "A tidbit you might enjoy is that Betty and Dean fell in love as teenagers. Her maiden name was Flowers. The shop's name is a takeoff of both their last names, a nod to their long-lasting love. I think it's sweet."

Ice had a different take on it. "What it is, is smart branding. No mistake about what they're selling."

Andrea popped the tailgate lock from a button on the dashboard. "I brought pie samples. They're in the back." As she reached for the door handle, her phone rang. She looked at the screen. "Molly."

She got out and walked around the SUV as she answered. Ice followed and began gathering the pie boxes from the trunk. She placed a hand on his, staying the action. "I see. Okay. I'm sorry. I don't know how that happened, but we're on our way. Be there in a few minutes."

"We have to go to the pie shop." She shoved the pie boxes back into place, slammed the tailgate, and hurried into the driver's seat.

"But what about our meeting?" Ice settled onto the passenger seat. "Aren't you going to let the Gardeners know you'll have to reschedule?"

"For some reason, Betty and Dean thought we were meeting at Big Sky Pie." She started the engine, backed out of the parking spot, and then roared across two lanes. "They're waiting for us there."

"So Molly had to tell them about the blueberries?"

"Yes, and she doesn't like delivering bad news."

*Who does?* "From the look on your face, I was thinking something more serious had happened."

She glanced at him as though she could read his mind and didn't like what she found there, like a complete lack of sympathy for anything that didn't relate directly to himself. He squirmed at the thought. She said, "Like the reporter being there looking for you?"

Exactly what he'd wanted to know, but now answering "Yes" seemed sort of like answering that question about an article of clothing making your woman look fat. Whatever he said, he'd be wrong, and he'd sound like a selfish, insensitive jerk. Normally he didn't care what anyone thought about him, but he cared very much that Andrea not think poorly of him.

He took a big swallow of the espresso and lied. "Bobby and Flynn are filming the contractor repairing the wall in the cold room. I thought maybe something had gone wrong."

"Bullshit. You thought Rita was there causing a ruckus. Admit it."

Damn, she could see right through him. "That might have crossed my mind."

She grinned at him, and the band around his chest loosened.

"Molly said it's been an interesting morning already. A couple of customers asked if they were on TV, and a couple of her gal pals came in and posed like models at a fashion shoot while ordering pie to go."

"The cameras are running in the café today." Ice laughed, picturing it. "Damn. I can't wait to see that footage."

"It's not funny. She's very upset."

He didn't believe it. Molly could roll with the punches. He studied Andrea for a moment, noting her white-knuckled grip on the steering wheel. "Are you worried about her heart? 'Cause according to her, she's back on her game."

Andrea glared at him. "You weren't here. You don't know how scary it was when she collapsed. You didn't see her with the light gone from those bright blue eyes, with her spirit dulled, and her voice so weak…"

Her voice hitched, and he spotted a tear spilling down her cheek. It stunned him into silence. He didn't think anyone loved him enough to shed a tear if he were to fall victim to a heart attack or even if he died. The knowledge settled like a black sore in his heart. He'd thought himself immune to the effects of love. He didn't like discovering that he wasn't.

They arrived at the pie shop. The Ice Berg Productions van was parked in back, beside Molly's car, Wade's pickup truck, and the other employees' vehicles. Andrea parked in front of the shop. She and Ice gathered the pie boxes from the cargo section of the SUV and hurried inside.

The delightful aromas filled his senses and calmed his anxiousness. The reporter was not here. The only customers were Jane and a beautiful older woman sitting in the front booth indulging in pie, tea, and conversation, while Molly was in the end booth with a white-haired couple who looked anything but happy. The Gardeners, Ice assumed. He set the pie boxes on a nearby table, then stood to the side as greetings and introductions were made.

The beauty with Jane was her mother, Rebel Scott, a wedding planner. Betty and Dean offered him a warm greeting, seeming able to momentarily set aside their personal disappointment and concern over the reception debacle.

Molly stood. "Betty and Dean, please excuse me for running out on you right now, but this is the first time I've let my assistant pastry chef handle the pumpkin pie filling for two dozen pies. I need to check on her and get those pies baking. But don't worry. Andrea is going to show you what we've come up with to replace the blueberry pies."

Dean said, "No problem." But Ice thought the waggling of his bushy brows proclaimed he didn't like being brushed aside.

Ice had left his venti in the SUV. He helped himself to a mug of coffee, listening to Andrea sounding confident and surefooted. She was in her element, he realized, seeing why Molly had insisted Andrea be the spokesperson for the reality show. She apologized to the Gardeners, hoped they'd understand that the freezer going out wasn't something anyone could have foreseen, and reassuring them that she and Molly had come up with several alternate options, one of which was bound to work for them.

"Oh, thank you, Andrea," Betty said. "I won't lie. We are disappointed, and a little worried. But it means a lot to Dean and me that we're dealing with friends and can have an open discussion and hopefully find a resolution."

"Everything is blue based on the blueberries," Dean grumbled, seeming less ready to move past the upset.

As Ice watched Andrea show them the options, he found it difficult to remember the Gardeners were senior citizens and not some young, newlywed couple. He'd shot dozens of pilots and directed several reality show series. He'd seen his share of so-called "in love" couples. None, to him, had seemed genuine. Oh, they talked the talk, used the usual hugs, kisses, and mushy nicknames, but they didn't walk the walk. Their eyes didn't light up just being in the same room with their spouse or significant other.

Over the years, he'd grown more and more cynical of *romantic love*—certain it did not exist—but was something made up for moviegoers. And yet here it was, right before his eyes. He felt as if he were viewing a magic trick that he knew was all smoke and mirrors, but he couldn't see the smoke, couldn't find the mirrors.

He snapped out of his musing when he heard Betty say, "We know that these things do happen. I don't want to be mad about it. It's enough that I have my Dean, you know? But I can't help it. I wanted everything to be so special."

Dean nodded. "Maybe we should go with cake after all. We can always have blue frosting."

Betty blushed as though she'd been caught considering an idea that was sure to hurt her friends, Molly and Andrea. But she said, "Maybe we should."

Andrea's face fell. Clearly she didn't want to lose this gig, and Ice didn't want that to happen either. If they went to another dessert shop, he wouldn't have the segment he wanted and needed for this pilot to sell. So he butted in just as the bell over the pie shop door sounded. Ice ignored it and began to sell the Gardeners on their possible involvement in the reality show.

"Ian!" Rita Grace shouted. "There you are."

Ice jerked around to see the reporter coming at him with a handheld recorder. Panic released a shot of adrenaline into his bloodstream. His only thought: escape. But the reporter stood between him and the café exit. He bolted behind the display cases, racing toward the workroom. In his mind's eye, he saw the route of escape as a clear shot through the kitchen to the back door. But as he shoved the first door inward, he met resistance, then a sudden, free-falling give. He pitched forward, catapulted with unstoppable momentum into the crowded workspace. Someone screamed.

Something wet and slimy slapped his face, followed by a cloud of white that seemed to be falling from the ceiling like an indoor snowstorm. Flour. It got in his hair, his eyes, his nose, blinding him, choking him. He scrubbed at his eyes, trying to focus, but before he could, something slammed into his head, quick, hard. He staggered, his legs going rubbery, and everything went dark.

## Chapter Eleven

⁓

By the time Andrea reached the kitchen, it looked like a war zone. Every surface, hard and human, had been dusted with flour and dripped with pumpkin pie filling. She caught sight of Rita outside, darting away between the parked vehicles, presumably still chasing after Ice, her dark hair bearing white skunk streaks.

BiBi was at the sink, swearing like a long haul trucker whose load had spilled across a freeway and looking like she'd been tarred and feathered in flour and pie filling. Molly cowered near the Sub-Zero, hand to mouth, eyes wide. Strangely, she was unscathed from the flying pie ingredients. Andrea asked, "What happened?"

"That's what I want to know." Molly shook her head. "I was getting something from the refrigerator. I heard the commotion, and when I shut the fridge door, this is what I saw."

Andrea glanced around again. Two large chunks of wallboard were teepeed in the center of the kitchen, and male voices issued from the hallway leading to the cold room. There, she found Bobby, helping Wade to his feet. Wade's tool belt hung askew, his baseball cap knocked off, and he had a disgruntled look on his face.

"Are you okay, man?" Bobby asked Wade.

"Nothing seems broken." Wade started to get up, accepting Bobby's offered hand.

"Do you guys know what happened?" Andrea inquired.

"Not me," Bobby said, shrugging. "I was setting up the lights and camera in the cold room to film the wall repair."

Wade reached for his cap, slapped it against his leg, and straightened. "I was bringing the sheet of wallboard in through the kitchen. Something slammed into it from across the room. The board shifted and pulled me with it, hit something else. I heard someone scream, but I was pitched off my feet, and I landed on my butt in the hall."

Andrea went back to the kitchen. BiBi was still swearing, but under her breath. She'd found a hand towel and was trying to clean the flour and pie goop from her face and hair. She met Andrea's gaze.

Andrea asked, "Do you know what happened?"

"Wade ran into me with his plasterboard." She sucked in a breath. "Molly had just poured the pumpkin filling into the pie shells and was getting ready to put them into the ovens. I was bringing a new sack of flour to the work island, and Wade was juggling a huge piece of plasterboard through the door. The next thing I know, the flour sack was ripped out of my arms, the paper split wide open, and flour exploded into a white cloud raining down like snow. Then I got knocked into the island and collided with all of the pies tins, flipping them over, spilling the filling, and sending the pans onto the floor." She swore again. "All those pies ruined. The kitchen ruined. Damn Wade anyway."

"It wasn't Wade," Andrea said.

"It wasn't?" BiBi's eyes narrowed, conveying a need to place the blame and exact revenge. "Then whose fault was it?"

"Ice Erikksen's. There was a reporter in the café. He was trying to avoid her, and he ran this way. He must have slammed the door into the plasterboard as he charged into the kitchen, heading for the back door."

"Well, he's going to pay for this mess when he shows up," Molly said, collecting pie tins from the floor and banging them on the marble counter.

Jane and her mother had come into the kitchen and were helping as well, but the Gardeners were standing in the doorway looking as though they wanted nothing more to do with Big Sky Pie. They met Andrea's gaze, shook their heads, and retreated into the café. She started toward them, the loss of their business slipping through her fingers like so much drippy pumpkin pie filling. She had to make them understand that broken freezers and accidents were mishaps that could happen to any business owner. Even them.

A quiet groan caught Andrea's attention, stopping her in her tracks. The wallboard teepee shifted, and a hand appeared. She gasped. "Someone's under there."

Wade scrambled to help her, lifting the plasterboard to reveal a man sprawled on the concrete, rubbing his head. Andrea dropped to her knees. "Oh, my God, Ice?"

Ice moaned again, his eyes blinking open, then closing as she and Wade helped him into a sitting position.

Ice said, "Anybody get the license number of that freight train?"

"It was that damned reporter, man," Bobby said. "Bitch wiped out the kitchen."

Andrea begged to differ. This mess was on Ice. He could have just talked to the woman or taken her outside the café door instead of running away.

"You okay, partner?" Bobby asked, hoisting a piece of wallboard.

"Yeah, sure. No sweat."

"Thank God for that hard head of yours."

"Yeah. Sure." Ice offered a weak smile as Wade and Bobby carted the broken wallboard away, carrying it outside.

"You're not okay," Andrea said, feeling a lump on the back of his skull. "You've got a bump on your head. Might be a concussion. Look at me."

He opened his eyes, his gaze seeming to take a moment to focus on her, but when it did, the intense blue was like a magnet drawing her nearer. A sweet, gentle thrum vibrated through her body in response. She tried to shake it off, to find the few nursing skills she possessed and ignore the female urges this man stirred in her.

But when her finger touched his face, she felt a sexual charge that had her pulling back. *Stop it. Check his pupils.* She gripped his chin, hoping he wouldn't notice the slight tremor in her hand, and peered closer. "Dilated unevenly. You need to see a doctor right away. I'll get Bobby to—"

"No." He caught her wrist. "You take me."

"What? No. He's your—"

"Please. He doesn't know anyone in town and, and you do."

As lame as she found this argument, she hesitated. A little boy vulnerability in his gaze reminded her of how Logan had looked when he'd admitted that he'd pushed his brother, an "I've done something bad, and I need you to understand, to be on my side" expression. Her heart and her resolve swayed. Ice didn't strike her as a man who easily asked for forgiveness and understanding. Or for help. But at this moment, he needed her. How could she refuse?

But Molly needed her, too. The pie shop, the Gardeners. Oh, damn, Betty and Dean. How could she explain this to them? A business could expect a bit more loyalty from friends than strangers, but even friends had their limit. The pie shop could be cleaned, but for all she knew, the Gardeners were already at a bakery ordering that blue cake.

She made a mental note to call them the first free second she had. Right now, though, Ice had to be seen by a doctor. Head injuries could be more serious than they seemed. Ice was trying to stand, leaning on her. Bobby and Wade returned, assisted him to his feet, then grabbed mops and buckets and began to help the women. Wade was apologizing to Molly and BiBi and Jane as if he had caused this mess.

Whereas the true guilty party, Ice, said, "I don't feel good." And hurled.

She had to get him to Emergency. She had an idea, though. She asked Bobby to put Ice into her SUV, then she pulled Rebel aside. "You're Dean and Betty's wedding reception planner, right?"

"I am."

"I guess you know how much this booking means to us. Not just for the business, but because they've become friends, and we're all almost as thrilled as they are that they've found each other again. Do you think you could ask them to hold off ordering a cake until I have a chance to speak to them and present what we've come up with as an alternative to the blueberry pies?"

Rebel's beauty queen smile presented itself. "Of course I will. After all, my Janey's pies should be the dessert for every life celebration as far as I'm concerned."

"Thank you." One less worry lifted from her shoulders.

She told Molly about driving Ice to Emergency, then turned around to leave and found a man standing in the café doorway. Her heart sank to her toes. Henry

Dolinski, health inspector, the walking definition of fastidious and persnickety, a tiny man with a large chip on his shoulder.

Henry held a clipboard to his concave chest, peering down his pencil nose and taking in the disaster in the kitchen, his thick lips pursed. "Ms. McCoy, this is most unacceptable. I'm afraid I'll have to write you up."

"Mr. Dolinski, Henry, your mother is one of my dearest friends, since before you were born. We play bridge together. Let me get you a cup of coffee in the café, and I'll explain what happened." Molly came toward him wiping her sticky hands on her apron, spotting it, and earning a nose wrinkling from the health inspector. "We had a mini-disaster about ten minutes ago. We'll have the kitchen spotless again in another hour or so. Meanwhile, we'll close the shop until it's sanitized again."

"Well, I should hope so." He started writing on his clipboard. "Close the shop, I mean."

Andrea knew she should stay out of it and let her boss handle Henry, but this was the last straw. "Can't you be a little understanding? What happened here won't ever happen again. It was a fluke."

"And how do I know that?" He stood as rigid as a brick wall. "Besides, I heard rumors a TV show was being filmed in this pie shop. Is that true?"

"It is," Molly said, urging him again to go with her into the café so that she could explain.

"I'm not sure you have the proper permits for that." Henry's chest puffed up like a rooster surveying his domain. She half expected him to crow as he stepped toward Molly, eyes narrowing with meanness. "I'll need to check with the head office as to whether or not that is in compliance with our regulations."

"We have the proper permits," Andrea told him. She'd taken care of obtaining them herself.

He ignored her as he sniffed the air like a cat detecting the scent of a nemesis. "What is that awful stench? Did"—and now his gaze zeroed in on Andrea—"did someone vomit in here?"

He glanced down. His polished wingtips were sole deep in puke. For half a second, Andrea thought Henry might lose his lunch. She stifled a grin, fearing she might actually laugh. But for him, this was too much. It sealed their fate. He whipped out his cell phone and videoed the calamity. "I'm going to a judge right now and getting an order to shut this shop down. Then I'll be back with an official closure notice, but I seriously suggest you lock the doors to this establishment immediately, Ms. McCoy." He reached for a paper towel to wipe off his shoes, gagged, and ran through the café, spreading vomit across that floor, too.

Molly, looking ready to spit nails, raced after Henry, pleading, cajoling, and finally shouting, "Henry Dolinski, I used to change your diapers."

She returned to the kitchen, steam boiling from her ears. "That pompous little prick. He was always a bully. I tried to warn Norma, but she wears blinders where that boy is concerned. I'm going to have to rip them off. Where's my phone?"

"I hate to interrupt, ladies," Bobby said, rushing in. "Andrea, I think you'd better get Ice to the doctor right away. He's feeling woozy and says his head is killing him."

*Oh, no.* "Molly, I have to get Ice to Emergency. I'll phone Quint and have him hire a cleaning crew. You go on home. BiBi can lock up and shut everything down for now. We can't do any more business today. Not since Henry spread the germs into the café."

"Do that, Molly. I'll help BiBi," Bobby volunteered.

Molly sighed. "You're right. If I stick around here, I'm liable to break something I care about. I need a shower, a nap, and then I'm going to have a nice, long chat with the mayor about one Henry Dolinski. But first I'm going to phone his mother."

Andrea didn't want to dash her boss's hopes by reminding her that the mayor worked for the town, but the Health Department was the county's domain. The mayor might not have any more influence over Henry Dolinski than they did, but his mother…that was another story.

* * *

All the way to the hospital, Andrea kept biting her tongue to keep from railing at Ice for his bone-headed move that might get Big Sky Pie shut down by the Health Department. But she couldn't verbally beat up on someone in his condition. She shoved her anger aside, calling up the few things she knew to do for someone with a head injury. Ask them questions.

Repeatedly. Her list included: "What day is this?" "What is the date?" "What's your name?" "Who is the president?" His answers were correct. She took that as a good sign, but still found herself chewing on her bottom lip.

"My skull feels like a surfboard slammed into it," he moaned, holding his head between his big, strong hands.

"I take it that has happened to you before?"

"A couple of times. Some waves will catapult you and the board."

The only things Andrea knew about surfing were that you needed great balance and that you risked being bitten by sharks. She shuddered. He could have the ocean; she'd take waterskiing on a lake.

Ice groaned again, holding his head, and panic nipped her, pressing her foot harder on the gas. "We're almost there."

She wasn't sure that painkillers were given for a concussion and decided not to mention that unless he brought it up. Déjà vu swept over her as she drove into the Emergency parking area and helped Ice to the check-in counter. This was her second visit here in the past few days, only this time it was not her child who was suffering, but a man that she hardly knew, a man she'd started to care for more than she wanted to.

They got Ice registered and took him right in. Andrea opted to stay in the waiting area, but as her worry receded, her anger returned. If he had just talked to that damned reporter...Men. What was with that fight-or-flight instinct? She'd thought Donnie invented it, but discovered over the years that it came imbedded in male DNA. Unfortunately, the fallout usually trickled down on innocent bystanders, like Molly, like her own sons.

If not for Ice's split-second decision to flee, Molly would have a kitchen full of cooling pumpkin pies, the wall in the cold room would have been repaired, the Gardeners would be happy with her solution to the ruined blueberries, and she'd be heading home to her sons.

But here she sat in the waiting area with no idea how long this was going to take, fighting the fear that Ice might be facing a more serious situation than it appeared. Damn. She did not like how worried she felt or that she was prepared to stay here as long as proved necessary.

She heard her phone vibrate. She'd missed a call from her mother. She needed to call her back and ask her to pick up the boys at the sitter's. But what reason could she give for the request? "I had to bring, er, ah, that guy you hoped I wasn't getting involved with to the hospital?" Or maybe she should lie. "I had to take a coworker to Emergency." And then her mother would ask which coworker and—since she knew them all— would be concerned. And once she asked *why* the coworker needed a doctor, she would have to explain the whole debacle at the pie shop. Just thinking about it gave her a headache, though nothing, she was sure, like the one Ice suffered.

She finally decided a fib was best. "Mom, it's me. I'm going to be delayed with work until really late tonight. Yes, it's about the reality show. Could you possibly pick up the boys and keep them overnight?"

"Of course I could. Would you rather I took them to your home for the night?"

"No." She didn't have anything there for dinner or breakfast. She'd planned on picking up some groceries after work. "I'd rather you be comfortable."

Her mother laughed. "Well, you won't believe this, but for some reason, I felt compelled to make a pot of mac and cheese this afternoon. And I picked up some pumpkin tarts at Big Sky Pie this morning. I didn't know what I was going to do with all this food, but I guess I do now."

*Someone is definitely looking down on me. Maybe I do have a guardian angel. Thanks, Daddy.* One of the knots in her stomach released, easing her tension a tad. "I love you, Mom. You're the best."

"Just don't work too hard, sweetheart."

As she ended the call, she heard her name. The nurse led her into the exam area to a curtained cubicle. Ice looked more vulnerable than he had when she'd brought him in, the hospital gown peeling away some of his usual tough-guy façade. "Thank God, Andrea. Will you please explain to this well-meaning doctor why I can't possibly stay the night here?"

It was more command than question. Andrea lifted her brows, glancing between Ice and the physician. "Does the doctor want you to spend the night?"

The doctor, a young female, nodded. "Mr. Erikksen has a concussion, and I've recommended he stay overnight for observation."

"I see." Andrea pinned Ice with a stern glance she reserved for obstinate fools. "And why are you objecting to this?"

"You know why. *That woman.* I don't want her to find me." The cryptic words were meant to eliminate the doctor's curiosity. It had the opposite effect.

The doctor said, "We can put a 'no visitors' notation on your chart, Mr. Erikksen." As if that would keep a determined investigative reporter from getting to a patient.

Ice groaned, silently pleading with Andrea. She could only imagine how vulnerable it must feel to be at the mercy of any fool with a camera or a smartphone. The price of celebrity. Not his fault; he'd been born into it. She pitied him that. But ignoring a doctor's recommendation wasn't advisable. He had a serious head injury. "Can he leave, Doctor, if he wants to?"

"He's not a prisoner, but I don't advise it, and if he does leave and has a problem later, his insurance may not cover—"

"Good." Ice tossed aside the sheet. "Hand me my clothes, Andrea."

She ignored the request. "What should he watch out for during the night then?"

"Dizziness, odd speech, or nonsensical dialogue. If his head pain increases. I'll have the nurse print you a list of instructions." The doctor departed, closing them in the curtained cubicle.

Ice grinned. "I thought she'd never leave us alone. My clothes, please."

Andrea did as he asked. "I'll go back to the waiting room, and you can meet me there."

A soft laugh, so throaty it made her toes curl, spilled from him, and his look pleaded with her. "I don't know if I can manage this on my own. I'm a little wobbly still."

"If you're wobbly, then you shouldn't leave."

"Are you going to help me?" He stripped off the hospital gown and let it drop. He was naked underneath. Her pulse skittered, and her insides turned all warm and slippery, tingling with anticipation. Damn, he was a pure delight without a stitch on.

"Is it the norm to run around naked in California? Or is this a personal trait of yours?"

"You didn't seem to mind the day we..."

She meant to lower her gaze, meant to keep her eyes on the floor, but how could she not admire such perfection? "At least you don't man-scape."

He placed his hand on her shoulder for balance and stepped into the striped boxer briefs, a smoldering light melting his blue eyes to the fiery glow of a butane flame. "Are you talking about on my chest, or...elsewhere?"

She knew she should be blushing, but she'd never been shy about her appreciation of the male anatomy, and she wasn't about to pretend now. "Everywhere."

"I'll make a note of that." He slowly pulled up the underwear, reluctantly hiding his goodies. "I think I'll need some help with my jeans."

He put both hands on her shoulders, leaning into her as he managed one leg then the other into the denim, then she tugged them up his strong, tanned legs, her own legs growing wobbly in this reverse striptease. When she reached the top of his thighs, he took over, adjusting himself with obvious difficulty given his arousal. "If you don't stop staring at me, I'll have to forget about buttoning my fly and do what we'd both like me to do."

She shook her head, laughing softly. "You're too sick for that."

"Honey, I'm never that sick."

# Chapter Twelve

~

Get your shirt on, surfer boy," Andrea said on a laugh, the sound as warm and inviting as waves crashing on the beach at his Malibu pad, as warm and inviting as her body. He fought the arousal that didn't want to be denied. The floor seemed to pitch beneath his feet like he was on a boat, bobbing on the Pacific.

She held the shirt toward him. "I'm taking you home."

"To bed?" Ice asked, hope in his voice. Damn, this woman was getting under his skin. It was all he could do to keep his hands to himself. Especially when he needed to lean on her so that the ground didn't reach up and grab him.

"Oh, you're definitely on your way to bed, but you'll be going there alone."

"That doesn't sound like any fun at all." His smile spread slowly across his face. "I've got the car ride to change your mind."

"That's so not going to happen."

He frowned, confused. "Did I just say that out loud?"

"Yes."

He shook his head, and pain shot across his skull. He stifled a moan, fearing she'd call a doctor and insist he not be allowed to leave the hospital. "Must be the concussion."

"You think?"

Once they were in the SUV and headed toward Front Street, he said, "By home, do you mean your place?"

"No. I mean your hotel suite. Bobby can take care of you tonight and make sure you follow these doctor's instructions." She handed the printouts to him.

"Well...that's one plan, but one that leaves me vulnerable to the wily Ms. Grace. What if she tricks a hotel employee into getting access to my room? To me? It's not like that hasn't happened to me before. More than once."

Andrea frowned, her expression thoughtful. "What did you do on those occasions?"

"Called hotel security."

"Then there you go." She offered him a smile. "Problem solved."

His head had started pounding again. "Yeah, but what if by the time security arrives, Rita has taken photos of me in my favorite state of undress and put them on the Internet?"

"Why would Rita do that?" She made a face, looking as skeptical as some network bigwigs he'd pitched pilots to over the years.

"Some gossip sites pay hefty fees for pictures of celebrity children. If she learns I was injured, she'll be on that like wax on a surfboard."

"Ha. How would she even find out about your concussion?"

"Reporters like her have ways of wheedling information from…unlikely sources." He rubbed his temples, trying to stem a sudden wave of pain. "Like any of the hospital staff who noticed me being led to an exam room."

Her skeptical expression said no one on the hospital staff had a clue who he was. "I think you're safe there."

"What if Rita somehow manages to get into the suite while Bobby and I are both asleep or away and steals all the film we've shot for the show?"

"Are you kidding me?" She started to laugh, and he knew he'd oversold it. "If you're worried about that, then maybe you should hire private security or put the film in the hotel safe."

He scowled, wincing at the new ache the frown elicited. "How about a plan B?"

"No. There's nothing wrong with plan A."

"But…I'm hungry, and, and I can't trust that room service won't let her into my room when they bring the food."

"Oh, for pity's sake. Okay, I'll take you to my place and fix you some chicken noodle soup and crackers, but if you can keep those down, I'm taking you back to the hotel. Understood?"

"Scout's honor."

"You were never a Boy Scout."

"True. But I wanted to be one." He'd wanted a lot of the things other boys took for granted like belonging to clubs, like playing high school football, like having loving parents. *"Don't settle for a tiny slice of the pie, son, not when you can have the whole bloody thing."* His father's unwelcome advice flitted across his mind, bringing another thought. "Hey, I'm sorry about what happened at the pie shop. Please make sure that Molly knows I'll pay to have it set right and cleaned."

Hesitation flicked through her beautiful brown eyes, accompanied by something that might be anger, but given his trouble focusing, he could have imagined that last.

She muttered something under her breath that sounded kind of like, "Even your father hasn't got enough money for that." But since that didn't make any sense, he decided it was a symptom of the concussion.

\* \* \*

"It's old, and it's not much to look at," Andrea told Ice as she helped him into her apartment, "but it's large and it's clean." She'd become a fanatic about germs when she was fifteen and her mother was going through chemo and radiation, her immune system compromised by those harsh cancer treatments, leaving Mom vulnerable to infection.

The compulsion also served her well during the time she, Donnie, and the boys lived in a trailer on the rodeo circuit, what with all the dust, dirt, and animal dung. Those years, she'd felt like she were a wheel rolling down a steep, bumpy road at someone else's whim. She'd needed to control something, anything, and cleaning became that thing. Donnie often complained about how rough or raw her hands were from all the scrubbing.

She felt Ice's breath on her neck, and it wrenched her back to the present with an awareness of a thousand sensuous shivers racing through her.

"I figured your home would be more...girly," he said, looking around, his arm still braced around her shoulders.

"What?" Andrea shook off his arm and stepped out of the danger zone. "Like all pink and frilly?"

His expression went vulnerable. He lost his balance and stumbled against her, pressing her to the wall, their noses less than an inch from touching, his eyes all needy. Her heart thudded against her ribs, her body melting into his, even knowing it was the worst thing she could do, that she was sending him all the wrong signals.

"What is it about you?" he asked, a question he'd asked her before, his voice a sensuous rasp. "Why can't I stop wanting you?"

"It's the concussion," she told him. "The desire will fade once your head is right again."

"Do you promise?"

"Yes." But the lie cut through her heart. This was

why she never brought men home. It was her space. Her safe harbor. The one place she could go when things overwhelmed her, where she could find the calm she needed in order to deal. But now Ice was leaving his stamp, marking his territory, almost imperceptibly. Long after he'd returned to Southern California, she would see him standing in her foyer, his broad shoulders filling the narrow hallway, his presence dwarfing the three chairs at the kitchen table, his larger-than-life persona imprinted on the walls of her once-private domain.

*What is it about him?* she wondered. She might have brought any other man here, and this would not be how it affected her.

She wrestled him as she might a drunk into a more upright stance and guided him into her small kitchen, settling him onto one of the chairs. "You should really be in bed."

"We should be." He reached for her hair, stroked a hand down her cheek, and Andrea's knees turned to butter.

She stepped away, grappling with her composure. "I thought you were hungry."

"I am. For you." Then he was on his feet, unsteady, reaching for her, pulling her into him, kissing her, banishing all the reasons why this wasn't just an awful idea, but a dangerous one. Not that her body had been listening to logic. It had a mind of its own, and it had taken total control, filling her with desire, the need so great she cried out his name.

Their lips were locked, his hands in her hair, as they moved backward through the apartment. She guided him to her bedroom. His kiss scrambled her reason, insanity ruling the moment, along with an irresistible, erotic craving. His intense blue gaze seemed to reach into her, the sensation like a burning branding, as though his soul were claiming hers, and her soul welcomed the possession.

He dropped onto the bed, pulling at her clothes and at his, awkward snatches and grabs until nothing separated them but their desire to explore with kisses, caressing, tasting. How could something be so wanton, yet feel so right? So forever? The thought melted away on another mind-bending series of kisses, his mouth torturing her nipples, her stomach, her inner thighs. His fingers found her moist, most sensitive spot and drove her to a devastating climax. Then just as quickly had her building to another.

Ice lifted himself over her, positioning himself between her legs, and lost his balance. He collapsed onto her, pushing the wind from her lungs. As he apologized, she began to laugh, and he joined her, the moment warm, wonderful, something funny shared by longtime lovers. She eased him onto his back, nibbled on his neck, and whispered in his ear, "Are you sure you can go on, surfer boy?"

As she sought his gaze for an answer, his eyes went from an intense ice blue to an electric shade like a butane flame. He grabbed her for another assault on her mouth, his tongue dipping inside to dance with hers, each stroke hotter than the last. Andrea sighed with pleasure, pushed him down onto the pillow, and tangled her fingers into the fine, silken hair on his chest as she licked his nipples into rock-hard nubs, then worked down his flat stomach, inching lower, then lower still. She teased the tip of his erection, quick, swiping licks, then took him into her mouth, deep and deeper, every plunge lifting her own need to new heights.

"Andrea," he rasped, clasping her upper arms, letting her know that his control had reached its limit.

She straddled him, and their eyes locked as they joined, the sensation exquisite. His rigid heat penetrating her sensitive, moist flesh almost undid her. Almost. With every thrust, her need found another pinnacle to aspire to, a higher high it wanted to reach, until that moment when she thought she could stand not another second of torture. Her body and mind tipped over into the land of ecstasy, falling and falling to a breathless, heart-thumping release.

She collapsed against Ice's chest, reluctant to disengage their bodies, just wanting to snuggle into the afterglow. He didn't push her away. He wrapped his arms around her, nuzzled her neck, and murmured soft, sweet, unintelligible words into her hair. Andrea settled into his embrace, praying this moment would never end.

And though it continued for several precious, tender minutes, it still didn't seem long enough. She rolled to his side, contentment easing through her as she settled on the pillow beside him.

"Was that what they call S and M?" Ice was clutching his head as if it might crack apart. "Pleasure and pain at the same time?"

"Oh, my God, I just tried to kill you. If I had a nursing license, it would be revoked."

"I willingly participated in that attempt on my life." A lopsided smile reached his eyes as he pulled her close, his palm cupping her bottom. "I'm okay, honest."

She could see where this was heading. Into round two. She seriously did not want to cause him injury. "You need to get some rest."

She climbed out of bed to his protests. "Be a good patient, and I'll fix you some soup."

She could tell he wanted to object more, but the effort was weak. He yawned, closed his eyes, and was fast asleep by the time she emerged from the bathroom fully dressed and still awash in the afterglow of their lovemaking. But this wasn't love. She and Ice were not falling for each other. And she had nothing to gain by continuing to sleep with him. She had to detach from him emotionally before she got hurt.

Her phone buzzed. A text from Quint.

Pie Shop is clean. Wade's fixing wall in the cold room in the A.M. Dolinski found a judge. Big Sky Pie officially shut down by Health Department until it is re-inspected. The little asshat is dragging his feet. Mama is working on mayor and Norma. How's our director's head?

Andrea texted him an update on Ice, then set about fixing herself something to eat, anything to soak up the anger she felt at that pompous little health inspector, and at herself for continuing to sleep with Ice. The pantry was pretty bare. Cereal, peanut butter, grape jelly, a box of salted crackers, and chicken noodle soup. She found a half-full bottle of wine in the fridge, poured a glass, and made a couple of sandwiches as the soup heated. Ice showed up as she was just finishing eating.

He'd dressed and seemed to be walking steadier. His hair was tousled from sleep, his jaw bristled with tawny whiskers, his gaze as warm as a summer sky. He smiled, gesturing toward the food. "It smells yummy."

"Yummy for your tummy." Andrea laughed. It was something she said to her boys about this particular meal. "Your appetite returning is a good sign that you're on the mend. Sit down. I'll serve you."

She'd already placed the second sandwich on a paper plate. He settled into the chair and reached for it as she asked, "What would you like to drink?"

"Water would be fine."

She placed a bowl of steaming soup before him, retrieved a bottle of water from the fridge, then returned to her chair and her wine. "Is your head still pounding? Or spinning?"

"More of a distant ache, like a throbbing you can't quite touch..." He dug into his pants pocket, withdrew a small red object, grinning as he set it on the table. "Um, I found this in your SUV this morning. Forgot to return it to the backseat."

Andrea stared at the toy sportscar. "It belongs to Lucas. He's into Nascar."

"Your son?"

"Yes." She nodded, deciding he might as well know it all so he could go running faster than he was going to anyway. "My youngest."

"There's more than one?" His eyes widened. The information obviously surprised him. Maybe he was wondering if there were *many* more than one. She wanted to tell him he had no reason to fret. She had no designs on him. She knew he wasn't a permanent kind of guy. But she answered his question with a nod of her head.

Ice took a bite of sandwich, followed by some water, then asked, "How many children do you have?"

"Just the two. Logan and Lucas. They're at my mother's for the night."

He frowned, wincing immediately in pain, telling her that the ache in his head was still pretty intense. He rubbed his bristled jaw. "And their father is..."

"Deceased."

Ice had reached for his sandwich, but the single word stayed his hand. Their eyes met. He searched her face, his look assessing, as though seeking some clue as to how much her sons' father had meant to her. He said, "I'm sorry. It has to have been hard on you and your two little boys."

Harder than anyone knew. Harder than she would tell him. "More so on the boys than me."

The assessing gaze continued. "Do you mind if I ask how..."

"I don't mind. Donnie was a champion bull rider. Always taking risks, always onto the next thrill."

"I'm sorry," Ice repeated.

"Don't be. Not for me. Lucas was three at the time, Logan five, but Donnie and I had divorced a couple of years earlier. He was onto his third bride, a barrel racer, younger, prettier, more exciting..."

"No."

"I beg your pardon?"

"She couldn't have been prettier or more exciting, not possible." The look in his eyes was fierce, as if he wanted to fight anyone who disagreed with him.

Something warm, like affection, meandered through her heart, chipping away at her composure. *Don't fall for Ice. Don't be in love with him. He's not the man for you or for your sons.* "Thank you, but I'm over it."

He lifted a skeptical brow. "Really?"

Okay, maybe betrayal was one of those things she might never put completely behind her, but she shrugged it off, not wanting Ice to know how sensitive she could be.

"I married Donnie Lovette for all the wrong reasons." Andrea shoved aside her empty soup bowl, leaned back in her chair, and explained about her mother's cancer diagnosis shifting her priorities. "I needed to grab hold of something alive and wild. I was too young to know the dangers of doing that and wouldn't listen when Dad tried to talk me out of it. I thought I knew more than he did."

Ice nodded. "Teenagers, huh?"

"Exactly. I was crazy about Donnie, obsessed maybe, but he cheated on me practically from the moment we exchanged our 'I dos.' He needed to prove his manhood all the damned time."

Ice winced as though she'd struck a nerve. "Some men are like that."

"At least you admit it." She smiled. "I knew it the moment I laid eyes on you."

This seemed to surprise him. "Then why did you sleep with me?"

"Ah, well, that's my flaw. I like men like you and Donnie. You're great in bed, and I haven't wanted anything more than that for a while now. Just the occasional tumble with a man who knows what he's doing, and who isn't a selfish lover."

"Thanks." Although he didn't seem to be taking this as a compliment. In fact, it seemed to make him sad. Or mad. "So there isn't a special guy..."

"Only my sons," she said, sipped some wine, and added, "but lately I've been thinking it's about time I did start seriously dating. Maybe I do want to fall in love and marry for all the right reasons."

"Marriage." He shuddered.

"Don't worry, I'm not talking about you."

*Now why did that seem to insult him?* He should be cheering. Probably some lingering concussion confusion.

"I'm glad we cleared that up," he said. "Because I don't want to mislead you into thinking what we did, that we, well, that it could ever be..."

Any secret hope she'd harbored that something between them might lead to a happy ending shriveled and died. She'd be damned, though, if he'd see how much what he'd just said hurt. *Change the subject, switch it to his life.* "What was it that went on with your parents, the big scandal Rita Grace mentioned that broke up your family?"

He glanced away from her, trailed his spoon through his soup, and avoided her gaze. "You could find that out on the Internet."

"I probably could, but I'd rather you told me."

# Chapter Thirteen

❧

Ice had never spoken to anyone about the awful thing he'd done that had destroyed his family, not to counselors, or schoolmates, or his business partner. The very reason he'd been hidden away was so that he wouldn't. Or couldn't. Just the thought of someone finding out filled the little boy he'd been with such shame that he'd banished the memory to a black hole somewhere deep inside. Any attempt to release the demon over the years brought on gut tremors and cold sweats.

He drew a ragged breath, bracing for the onset of the usual symptoms, followed by a complete emotional shutdown, but after a minute of pretending he hadn't heard Andrea's request, the only thing he felt was a slight trepidation. No internal shudders. No sweaty palms and clammy skin. Andrea sipped her wine, glancing at him, giving him time to figure out whether or not he could open up to her. Damn. What was it about her that he was even considering telling her?

Was it the compassion in her voice when she spoke about her sons? Or his feeling that she was the mother he'd wanted his mother to be? A mother who wouldn't blame a child for an adult's betrayal? Or maybe it was how open and honest she was. He heard himself saying, "It was my seventh birthday. My father gave me a kid's digital camera. It was the single greatest gift I've ever received. I'd always wanted to be a director, you see, like my daddy."

Andrea tilted her head to one side, listening, a tiny smile in her eyes as if she were imagining him as a boy, receiving the gift of a lifetime.

Ice's gaze snagged on a tiny drip of wine near the corner of her luscious mouth, at her tongue darting out to catch it. Desire distracted him for a moment until she asked, "What did you photograph?"

The question brought him back to his story, and he hesitated. His mouth felt as dry as the flour in the bins at Big Sky Pie. The first part was easy; the next was his undoing. He took a gulp of water, telling himself to rip off the bandage. Get it out. All of it. "I was pretending that I was shooting locales for my big, upcoming film. I wandered all over the mansion and grounds, snapping anything that struck my fancy." He took another pull from the water bottle. "I even went out by our Olympic-sized pool—which I was strictly forbidden to go near on my own—and sneaked into the pool house."

To this day, every time he heard Whitney Houston's "I Will Always Love You," it threw him back to that moment. "My dad was there with, I thought, my mother."

He watched Andrea leap ahead mentally, already connecting the dots. "Oh, no." He didn't deny or confirm. A lump formed in his throat, and he feared if he stopped the story right now that he wouldn't finish. "The door into the dressing room was open a crack, and their reflections filled the big mirror over the bar. They were *wrestling* on the floor of the dressing room. I was seven, sheltered, and didn't realize what was actually going on. I snapped a few shots. Then bored with that, I went back outside and on to more interesting exploring and picture taking, a wild rabbit eating Mother's prized roses, the butler washing Daddy's car—in my imagination a spy toying with the brakes.

"Later that evening, I begged my mother to put the photos I'd taken on the computer. Even though she was still getting ready for her trip, I knew she'd do it. She'd always indulged me, saying that she couldn't deny me anything because I looked so much like my daddy, and besides, it was my birthday."

Andrea seemed to sense how difficult this next part would be. Her hand covered his, and the warmth seeped into him, letting him know he wasn't taking this journey into the past by himself. He didn't have to face the old demon alone. He didn't let anyone get close. Not ever. Somehow this sexy blonde whom he'd known for such a short time had slipped through the moat and over the castle walls to touch him emotionally, to make him care about her.

"You don't have to tell me the rest if it's too painful."

"No, I want to tell you. I want you to know."

"Okay."

He cleared his throat, trying to dislodge the lump. "As you've no doubt guessed, the woman with Daddy wasn't my mother. It was my nanny." The ache in his head returned with a swift arc across his skull. "I didn't understand the sexual implications, of course, I just knew my parents were screaming at each other, and that it was my fault. Daddy left the house after telling me that I had ruined our family and robbed him of his Golden Ticket."

Andrea gasped. "He told you that? He blamed you for *his* indiscretion?"

"He did. I didn't understand any of it. I ran crying to my mother, but she was too wrapped up in her own devastation and couldn't bear to look at me. The thing she'd loved, my resemblance to my father, was now my curse."

"Oh, my God. Excuse me if I don't like your parents. How could they do that to you? Logan resembles his father, too, but that's not his fault, and it doesn't change how much I've always loved him. He's not Donnie. You weren't responsible for your dad's mistakes You didn't betray your mother."

It was the first time anyone had gone all warrior woman on his behalf, and the effect was startling. A fissure cracked across the frozen plain covering his heart, splintering the icy shell. A tiny rivulet of something warm slipped through the rift to pool deep inside him. He was disoriented and rattled at this new development, but the feeling didn't leave and seemed to be growing stronger, warmer.

He scooted his chair back and stretched his legs. "The family lawyers stepped in. I was whisked off to a private boys' school, my name legally changed in an effort to keep me off the radar of reporters and newscasters looking for a scoop."

"Both of your parents walked away from you? At age seven? On your birthday? That is so many kinds of wrong, I can't even find words…" Her face was crimson with fury, her eyes full of disbelief and sorrow and pity.

The last wasn't something he wanted. Not from her. "Please, don't pity me. Pity is a useless emotion. I know. I've spent a lifetime feeling sorry for myself."

"No one had a better right." She shook her head. "Have you reconciled with either of your parents?"

They had reached out to him over the years, but he'd kept his distance. He couldn't bridge the chasm of the lost years; he didn't need his parents any more than they needed him. They'd both remarried several times and had other children, a half-brother and two half-sisters that he'd never met. Including Ariel Whittendale. "No, I…"

That seemed to infuriate her even more. "I can't believe a mother would—" She broke off, seeming to realize she was rubbing salt into the wound, hurting him. It did still hurt, but the pain was as much a part of him as his blue eyes. "Why did you even move back to California when you graduated?"

"My granddad, the one whose last name I was given, left me a ton of money, which I inherited when I turned eighteen, along with a beach house in Malibu. It was one of the few places that held nothing but happy memories for me. I moved in and remodeled it."

"I've never even seen the Pacific Ocean in person."

"It's amazing."

"I'll take your word for that. So how did you end up back in the movie industry if you were avoiding your dad?"

"I never got over the desire to be a director. I met Bobby at UCLA's School of Theater, Film and Television. We hung out together. Surfed. Kicked back. Then one day, he suggested we should start our own company. I liked the idea of making my own mark in the same industry as my parents." *Thumbing my nose at them.* Ice yawned, and pain split across his head again. If he didn't lie down soon, he would fall down. Telling Andrea about his childhood woes had drained the last of his energy. He shoved aside his half-eaten sandwich. "I need to lie down or I'll pass out in my soup."

"I should take you to the hotel."

"I'll be lucky to make it down your hallway." He wanted to crawl back into her bed and spend the night with her wrapped in his arms, but now he recognized how selfish it would be to take advantage of the protective instincts he'd roused in her. She wasn't like any woman he'd ever met. She wasn't after fame. Or fortune. She didn't count happiness by the numbers in her bank account. She was what he'd been looking for his whole life and had come to believe didn't exist—an honest, genuine person. Someone he didn't need to lie to about who he was. Someone who liked him for himself. Warts and all.

Unfortunately, he didn't deserve that kind of woman. He was a rolling stone, better off without ties or anchors. Free to do whatever appealed at the moment. And at this moment, she appealed more than he could control. But he had to. For her sake. She wanted a husband, a father for her kids. He wasn't that man. And she would only be hurt if he pursued this unrelenting desire he felt for her, if he let her start to care about him, if he started to care about her. "Would you let me crash on your couch, please?"

She blinked, looking surprised, and maybe disappointed by the request. She gathered the dishes from the table and put them into the sink. "You can sleep in Logan's room. He's tall for his age, and I got him a regular-sized bed for him to grow into."

She dried her hands and offered to help him.

"I can manage," Ice said, afraid if she touched him that his resolve would melt away and they'd end up in bed. Reminding himself that not making love with her was the best thing for her, he followed on wobbly legs as she led him to a bedroom across from the hallway bathroom. The walls were painted dark blue with stars on the ceiling, and the large twin bed had a spaceship bedspread and sheets. She snatched a pile of clothes from the floor, apologizing. "Logan is the messy one."

Ice smiled. "If I can tolerate Bobby's slovenliness, I can manage one night in here."

As soon as she left, he shucked his jeans and climbed into the bed in his boxer briefs and T-shirt and was asleep moments after his head touched down on the pillow. He vaguely recalled Andrea checking on him once or twice during the night. Doctor's orders, he presumed.

When he finally opened his eyes, morning light spilled through the thin curtains. For several moments, he felt that disoriented sense of being in an unfamiliar space, of not knowing where exactly he was or what day it was. Not a hotel room. The bed wasn't as wide as he preferred. He had a hard-on from dreaming all night about a blond temptress, and from waking up wanting her. He sensed someone else in the room. He turned in anticipation, expecting to meet a pair of beautiful brown eyes and a heart-stopping smile.

Instead, the gaze that met his belonged to an irate, blue-eyed kid with dark hair. His erection fizzled.

"Who are you?" the boy demanded. "Why are you sleeping in my bed?"

Ice stretched and grinned as he recalled exactly where he was. "I'll bet you're Logan."

"Maybe." He grew leery. "What'd you do with my mommy?"

"What?" Ice tossed back the covers and swung his legs off the bed. "Isn't she here?"

Logan leaped back, eyes wide. "Grammy!"

* * *

Big Sky Pie looked as normal as any other day except for the hateful Health Department Closure placard in the window. Andrea let herself in, locking the door behind her. Instead of the aromatic fragrances that usually met her—fruits and spices and the earthy scent of dough—there was an underlying odor of disinfectant. It was a smell she knew well. But there was also the rich aroma of fresh-brewed coffee, and after the night she'd had, she might need the whole pot.

Maybe she shouldn't have walked out and left Ice there by himself, but she couldn't face him this morning. He'd poured his heart out to her, shared his most painful secret, broke every protocol of the one-night-stand ethic: *No emotional involvement.* She'd ached for him after hearing what his parents had done to him, had taken him into her heart as she would a man she loved. She'd crossed the line into a serious, no-going-back bond with him.

By choosing not to spend the night in her bed, he'd made it clear that he didn't want her to care about him in any permanent way. Why did that hurt so much? She'd known how he felt all along, and yet somehow she'd thought…Oh, hell, she'd spent half the night trying to figure out what she thought. She didn't want Ice. She did want Ice. *I love him, I love him not.* The end result was that her common sense had declared war on her emotional reasoning, and she was more confused than ever.

She took a long sip of coffee, welcoming the hot punch through her middle, the sudden jolt of caffeine. A vision of Ice filled her mind, but it was not the image of him asleep in Logan's bed with the astronaut bedspread tucked under his chin. Instead it was the way he looked at her as they were making love, the way he'd clung to her afterward as they recovered from their breathless joy. This haunted man had touched her heart, had claimed a part of her that would forever belong only to him.

That was the real reason she'd left him alone. With the concussion subsiding and his rational thinking restored, he might regret having opened up to her, so she'd given him the chance to walk away without any obligation or explanation or regret. He could always get a ride back to his hotel by phoning a cab or his partner.

As she made her way to the coffee counter, she heard voices coming from the depths of the pie shop. The cold room maybe? Or the office? She carried her mug into the kitchen. Molly and Quint sat at the work counter, heads together, deep in discussion. Every surface in the kitchen, from cabinet to appliance to floor, gleamed, not one sign that it had ever looked any other way.

Quint gave her a cockeyed grin. "Lovette."

"Good morning, dear." Molly looked up, a smile of welcome lighting her eyes. "How's Lucas doing?"

*Considering all she must be dealing with, Molly's first concern is for me and mine? Amazing. I want to be just like her when I grow up.* "A little better every day. Thanks for asking."

Andrea set her purse on the work island and grabbed a stool. She had a couple of incredible older women in her life. Her mom had been taking the boys to school when she'd checked in this morning, and now this. She took a sip from her mug, glancing from one McCoy to the other over its rim. "So what's going on? Anything new since last night?" She directed this last to Quint.

"Mama and I are trying to figure out what to do with the pies in the cases and the ones in the refrigerators." He ran a hand through his collar-length, blue-black hair, his expression one she recognized. He was all business at the moment, concentrating on fixing whatever wasn't working. "They're perishable."

"But the kitchen is spotless. Why hasn't Henry shown up and signed off on the reopening?" Andrea had checked into the procedure. "The judge who okays a closure like ours also gives the Health Department the authority to sign off on our reopening."

"That little shit." Quint had an "if I get my hands on him" scowl. "He isn't answering our phone calls."

Anger burned through Andrea's stomach. How dare Dolinski pull this? It was unprofessional and mean. He was tarnishing their reputation with this shutdown. "It's not like we had cockroaches or rats or *E. coli*. It was a damned series of mishaps. An accident. That can happen to anyone. I will hunt him down."

"And hang him from the nearest tree? 'Cause I'll bring the ladder," Molly said on a little laugh, though Andrea suspected she meant it. At least at this minute. "Oh, dear, I completely forgot to ask, how is Mr. Erikksen? Did he have a concussion? Have you heard anything more about how he's doing?"

Andrea's cheeks heated with embarrassment for how much she knew about Ice's medical condition. She fiddled with the clasp on her purse, not gazing directly at either Quint or Molly. "He suffered a slight concussion, but nothing so serious that he had to stay the night in the hospital." Nothing so serious he couldn't make love. Nothing that had kept him from trying for another round or two during the night every time she'd gone into Logan's room to check on him. "I, er, haven't seen or spoken with him today, but I'm assuming he's fine. Oh, and don't worry about the loss of the merchandise. Ice said he'd pay for whatever damage he'd incurred since this was his fault."

"Well, money won't get that runt Dolinski to return our calls and give us the go-ahead to reopen," Quint groused. "Or, trust me, the doors would already be open."

"Henry must be a very unhappy man." Molly actually seemed sorry for the guy. "He derives such pleasure from being mean."

"Maybe celebrity power would help," Andrea heard herself suggest.

"Well, so far the mayor's pleas have fallen on deaf ears," Quint said. "He won't even return his mama's calls."

"Norma is fit to be tied," Molly added.

"I'm not talking local celebrities, I'm talking the Hollywood variety." At their questioning frowns, Andrea explained who Ice's parents were.

"No shit," Quint said. "You wouldn't know it by talking to him."

"His not flaunting it makes me like him more," Molly said.

"I doubt his being famous will help the situation." Quint sighed. "Henry isn't starstruck by anyone but himself."

"It was just a thought." A thought that led her straight back to Ice. She didn't want to think about him anymore. She clutched her coffee mug with both hands, letting the warmth soak in and calm her. "I noticed Wade's pickup out back. Is he here?"

Quint nodded, his hair flopping onto his forehead. "Just applying the taping mud to the plasterboard. He claims it'll be good to go by the end of the day."

"Molly, has anyone spoken to the Gardeners?" Andrea's brain was keying in on things that needed to be seen to, calls that needed to be made. "I haven't been able to reach them, and I thought maybe they might have phoned you?"

"No, dear. Trying to reach Henry has been a full-time chore today."

"Well, I'll try again. And I'll make some other calls about the pies. I'm wondering if the homeless shelter could use several as well as the diner I told you about. Don't worry, I'll come up with a few more places and then start delivering them."

Andrea started toward the office, then stopped. She had to get over Ice, and the best way to do that was to move on, to put in motion her find-a-stepdaddy plan.

Starting here and now. She screwed up her courage and marched into the cold room. Wade was standing framed against the bright light, admiring his handiwork.

He glanced around at the sound of her boot heels on the concrete floor. "Hey, good morning."

"Good morning yourself." She gestured to the wall. "All done?"

"The tape needs to dry, but that'll take a couple more days." He began gathering his tools, a sexy guy in blue jeans and western shirt, a touch of white taping mud in his dark hair. "By the time this place is reopened, it'll be just like the leak never happened."

"Wonder if Charlie Mercer has figured out the cause of the freezer dying."

"Wouldn't know." He shrugged. "Where are the cameras today?"

She had no idea and didn't care. It was nice not to have the extra chaos. "I think they've done enough damage for a while. I hope they don't show up today. Nothing going on anyway."

He held his taping mud tray, gazing down at her, the moment awkward, stilted. She wanted to ask him out, but she didn't ask men out. They usually asked her. Wade was shy, old-fashioned. He might think she was overstepping.

As though he'd been reading her mind, he blurted out, "I've been thinking... would you like to go to dinner later this week?"

He seemed as surprised that he'd asked as she was to hear the question. She wanted to get to know him bet-

ter, so it was nice to know he could step up if he had to.
"I would."

"Great. How about Friday at Moose's? Or if you'd
rather, we could go somewhere fancier."

"For a first date, Moose's would be perfect." Familiar ground for them both, the prices were reasonable,
and the atmosphere wasn't too intimate or suggestive,
in case the chemistry she felt with Wade turned out to
be nothing more than a case of nerves.

She wished him a great day and went to the office to
get started on her calls. She phoned several places who
were more than happy to receive free pies, and a few
who insisted on paying for them. Almost every person
she spoke to commiserated with Big Sky Pie over *that
awful Henry Dolinski.* So many folks seemed to share
this opinion that she started to wonder if they could
initiate a petition to get him placed somewhere in the
Health Department that didn't wield so much power.

She spent the afternoon delivering pies, silently willing the Gardeners to return her calls. She tried Rebel
Scott, too, hoping for an update from that source, but
she didn't answer. Frustration tensed Andrea's muscles,
giving her the start of a headache. She hadn't heard
from Ice either. She hadn't expected to, but she was
surprised he hadn't at least phoned Molly once he'd
learned about his part in the pie shop being shut down
by the Health Department. She'd resisted sending him a
text. She had accepted a date with Wade. She was moving on. Doing what she had to do to overcome her bad-
boy obsession. Seeking a better life for herself. For her

sons. She also knew she didn't dare take another step in Ice's direction. She was *almost* in love with him, but falling over that precipice would be the end of her.

Her mom texted to say she'd taken the boys home and would wait there until Andrea arrived. She stopped at the store to pick up groceries and the latest animated DVD. Tonight, she planned to fix the one meal she couldn't screw up—spaghetti, applesauce, and salad. Molly McCoy's pie was for dessert with some ice cream. The boys were going to be thrilled. After the dishes were done, they would snuggle on the couch, watching the movie with, maybe, some buttered popcorn. If they weren't all too full. She smiled to herself as she drove home. Things were looking up, looking toward a new and different future. One that was long overdue.

Juggling grocery bags, a pie box, and her purse, Andrea opened the apartment door. The unmistakable aroma of sautéing onions and peppers greeted her. Darn it, she should have texted her mother not to start dinner. "Mom, you didn't have to—"

The words froze on her tongue. Ice stood at her stove, one of her aprons wrapped around his waist, stirring something in her best frying pan. And her sons and her mother were all helping him.

# Chapter Fourteen

Andrea set her groceries on the kitchen counter with a thump. "What's going on?"

Everyone turned at once, surprised to find her there. They all spoke at the same time.

"Sweetheart," her mother said.

"Hi," Ice said, looking glad to see her, as though finding him cooking dinner were the most natural thing in the world.

"Mommy," Logan said, grinning from ear to ear.

"Mommy, Ize is letting us cook," Lucas said, bubbling over with excitement. "He teached us about sauting unyums."

Andrea raised questioning brows at her mother.

Delores started talking fast. "School let out after half a day. Some teachers' meeting or other. Logan said he forgot to give you the notice. When they called, I picked up the boys and brought them here. After what went on in the pie shop yesterday, I didn't want to bother you at work."

"Logan found Ize in his bed," Lucas said, always the informant.

She expected Logan would give her some grief over this, but he was gazing at Ice like she'd caught herself doing. What the hell? Logan was the mistrustful one, but Ice had apparently won him over. Not an easy task. Logan was acting like they were long-lost buddies. Had she walked into some Twilight Zone alternate reality?

Logan seemed more...confident? Was that possible in a few hours? He shifted his weight, acting cool. "Ice took us to the park. We played catch with my football. It was awesome. He taught me how to hold it with my ring and little fingers crossing the laces and my thumb underneath, like this." He snatched the football off the table and demonstrated, then recited as though he'd memorized the rule. "My index finger should be over a seam. My thumb and index finger should make an L shape."

The joy in her son's voice zinged straight to her heart. She couldn't remember the last time he'd seemed so happy. It drove home how much her sons needed the influence of a man to teach them things she and her mother just didn't know about, like the proper way to hold a football. But Ice was a stranger. Her boys had only met him today. What was her mother thinking allowing him to take off with her children? "You shouldn't have."

"Ah, it was no trouble," Ice said, totally misreading her statement. "I had as much fun as the boys. Maybe more." God, he was beaming like Logan. Hadn't anyone played football with him as a kid? His story and circumstances came rushing back, and she realized they probably hadn't, and the knowledge made her sorrier for him, softening her resistance.

She gave herself a mental slap. "That's not the point."

He studied her, obviously trying to discern the root of her quiet anger, and then a mental light seemed to click on. He threw up his hands and shook his head. "No, no. Your mother chaperoned our whole afternoon."

As if that made this okay. "I see."

"We wanted to get to know Ice better." Her mother gave her a pointed look, as though she had meant to find out more about the man that she felt her daughter might be falling for, the Donnie Lovette clone. She didn't appear to disapprove of Ice. In fact, if he hadn't been standing here, Andrea feared Mom might give her a thumbs-up.

Andrea groaned to herself. Here she was trying to oust this man from her life, and her whole family was embracing him, falling for that celebrity charm.

"The boys confided to me that you aren't as good a cook as your mom."

"I like your peanut butter sandwiches," Logan said quickly.

"Yeah, me too," Lucas chimed in.

"Me three." Ice smiled that heart-stopping grin. "They were surprised to learn that I like to cook."

He cooks? What? He wasn't dreamy enough already before she knew he could cook? Why had fate delivered the perfect man into her life when she couldn't have him? Had she been really bad in some other lifetime to deserve this punishment? She pulled open the fridge to put away her groceries and found it completely stocked. Milk, bread, butter, eggs, salad makings, fruit. "So you took Mom and the boys grocery shopping?"

"Yeah, I noticed you were low on a few things."

Low was such an understatement that she almost choked. There was even bottled water and white wine stowed on the side shelves, and five beers left of a six-pack. She didn't drink beer. Neither did her mother. Did he plan to stick around and finish the rest? She just stared at him, uncertain if she was angry or grateful, or both.

Ice fixed his incredible gaze on her. "I decided to teach the boys a few culinary tricks that they can teach you. You know, later."

*Yeah, later, when you're gone.* A wayward stab of pain breeched her heart. Damn him. It was bad enough that she would miss him when he left, but now her sons would miss him, too. Maybe even her mom would miss him. *Angry. Definitely more angry than grateful.* This was why she didn't bring men home.

Since she couldn't insist he leave with dinner under way or vent to either Ice or her mother with the boys present, she decided if she couldn't beat them, she'd join them. She poured herself a glass of wine, handed Ice a second beer, and stood by the stove to see what they were preparing. Some sort of pork chops.

Maybe it was the wine plucking at her wall of resistance, but she felt herself mellowing and enjoying the happy chatter and camaraderie that came with cooking a meal together. The kitchen space was tight. Several times, she brushed up against Ice as she gathered dishes and set the table. Twice their hands bumped, their eyes met, and an electric pull charged through her.

Lucas chattered nonstop about everything as if he sensed he would only have this male attention for a limited time, and he intended to get as much out of it as was humanly possible. She would have reined him in, but Ice was so gentle that she couldn't do that to either of them. She knew instinctively that Ice needed this as much as Lucas did, even if Ice didn't realize it. This whole new side of him threw her.

Gone was the bad boy, Mr. One Night Stand who'd strolled into Big Sky Pie hiding behind aviator glasses and a doesn't-give-a-shit attitude. If she held up a mirror, he wouldn't recognize his own reflection. There was more to this man than anyone knew, more than he'd ever shown the world, or himself. It wasn't Ice standing in her kitchen; this was Ian. And she marveled at how much she cared for both of them.

Dinner was a pure delight. The boys were thrilled that they had helped make it. She would have to include them more whenever she cooked. Maybe she should take a cooking class. Nothing too fancy. Just enough to learn a few things. Maybe she and Mom could take the class together.

After dinner, her mother helped with the dishes, then

announced that it had been a long day and she was going home. The boys insisted Ice stay for the movie. Andrea could hardly object. As Logan readied the DVD, she went back to the kitchen to make the popcorn.

Ice came in. "Can I help?"

"Nothing to do." She placed a bag of buttered popcorn into the microwave and set the timer. She found the big bowl they used for movie night and set it on the counter, aware of Ice's gaze on her every movement. She needed to cut the sexual tension between them. "Did you know that, after the fiasco in the kitchen yesterday, the Health Department shut down Big Sky Pie?"

"Yeah, Bobby texted me. I phoned Molly and Quint, and I'll make up any loss of revenue to them as well as pay for all the cleaning. I know that won't compensate for any loss of clientele due to this closure, though." He looked so sorry, her anger waned.

"Well, I think we'll be okay. I found out a lot of folks in town have fallen victim to Henry Dolinski's bullying tactics. His boss could be about to receive a hundred or so complaint letters about him."

Ice smiled, and her insides began to melt into hot lava. She wanted to touch him, wanted him to touch her, wanted him to pull her close and kiss her. She pulled her gaze from his, retrieved the popped bag of corn from the microwave, and filled the large bowl.

"That smells delightful," he said, bringing her gaze to his.

"That's what you said the first time we met."

"I was talking about the popcorn this time."

"I know." She put another bag into the microwave.

He braced his hip against the counter. "I wanted to tell you that I'm leaving."

Her heart dropped to her toes, and she struggled to keep her face from reflecting her dismay. "Oh? The pilot's done then. When are you going?"

"Tomorrow. But it's the show that's done. Molly and Quint decided to call off the pilot. They feel the reality show is too disruptive, not nearly as much fun as it looks on TV."

Andrea had been involved with Molly's attorney when the contract between Ice Berg Productions and her boss was drawn up. She knew a clause or two had been included to cover this possible outcome. But it wasn't her only concern.

"What about the studio that commissioned the pilot? Won't there be some sort of financial loss that someone would have to absorb?"

"They have insurance for that, but in this case, we had a private investor. Anonymous. He came forward as soon as I texted to tell him the pilot was a bust. It turns out it was BiBi's father, Chopper Henderson. He wanted her to be the star of the show. Or at least have the most TV time. He's also the one who sicced the press on me, figuring some media attention might help the pilot sell."

"He would. He misses the limelight. BiBi misses living in Hollywood, but she's a daddy's girl, and Daddy lives in Kalispell." This was, however, as far as Andrea knew, the single nicest thing BiBi's father had done for her.

"Yeah, well, she and Bobby have been hooking up. If you get a chance, you might want to warn her that he's in major rebound mode. Just coming off a nasty divorce."

"BiBi's got a mind of her own." And a tattoo that said *Defiance*. "Whoever she hooks up with is not going to be influenced by me." Andrea recalled seeing BiBi in Moose's with Bobby. It looked like she wouldn't be the only one brokenhearted when Ice Berg Productions left town.

"Just thought someone should know."

"I guess you'll be needing to get back to the hotel to pack up." *Cut the strings that have tried to wrap you up all evening. Cut them quick. Ruthlessly.*

He frowned. "The boys wanted me to stay and watch the movie."

"You know, that's not a good idea." She pulled the second bag of popped corn from the microwave and emptied it into the big bowl. "I thank you for spending so much time with them today, but you won't be seeing them again, and kids tend to get attached too quickly. It would be best if you—"

"Ize, are you coming or not? Logan is gonna start the movie."

Ice glanced at Andrea. She sighed, and jammed the popcorn bowl into his arms.

During the movie, Andrea sat with Lucas curled against her side, but her gaze kept wandering to Ice. She'd caught him staring at her, a longing look in those dreamy eyes. Was he thinking that he might miss her as much as she was going to miss him? She tore her gaze from him, pushing down the yearning inside, forcing herself to stare at the TV.

Lucas sat up suddenly and interrupted her thoughts. He glanced at her, then at Ice, then said, "Get a room."

Andrea startled. Had her six-year-old just said "get a room"? "What?"

Logan was giggling. Ice, too, looked amused.

"Well, that's what they say on TV," Lucas explained, "whenever some guy and lady are making moony eyes at each other like you and Ize are doing."

Embarrassment flushed her skin.

Ice looked chagrined.

Lucas asked, "What does it mean?"

Andrea asked, "What does what mean, sweetie?"

"Get a room."

Ice put his hand to his mouth, and Andrea knew he was hiding a grin.

Logan giggled harder as if he knew exactly what the expression meant. Lord, did he? At least sort of? Was it time she told the boys the facts of life? Weren't they still too young? If Donnie had been here, she had no doubt he would do it. But she wasn't Donnie, and she wanted her sons to remain as innocent as possible for as long as was realistic.

Another reminder that a man in her life, in their lives, was much needed.

"Mommy, what does it mean?" Lucas persisted.

"Did anyone ever tell you that you ask too many questions?"

Logan jumped into the conversation. "My teacher

says that, if you don't know the answer to something, asking a question is the only way to learn."

"Your teacher's right, Logan," Ice interjected. "But in this case, it just means that no one wants to see the guy and the lady being mushy. You know, like go into the other room."

"Oh," Lucas said, reaching for more popcorn and immediately reengaging in his movie.

Logan joined him on the sofa, yawning, his football tucked to his side like one of the stuffed animals he'd lugged around everywhere not so many years ago. Andrea mouthed a "thank-you" to Ice.

The movie ended shortly after that, and Andrea sent the boys to brush their teeth and get their jammies on. Alone, she carried the popcorn bowl to the kitchen.

Ice followed. "They're wonderful children. You've done a terrific job raising them."

"Yeah, well, sometimes it would be nice not to have to do it all alone, as you saw tonight."

He nodded. "They need a man in their lives who isn't going anywhere. And for the first time in my life, I wish I could be that man. For them. And for you."

*I wish you could be, too.* "I think these feelings we share are confusing and pretty wonderful, but it's not the lasting, forever-after kind of thing. We recognized a kindred spirit in each other. That is very seductive. We've both known someone who was supposed to love us, but who didn't, and unless you've lived that, you don't understand. But those betrayals came at a price, leaving us both wary of commitment."

She didn't give him a chance to respond, but plunged ahead. "I have realized, if I continue making the same choices, I will always end up alone and lonely. So I'm going to make some positive changes in my life."

He was frowning so hard she thought it must hurt. "Changes?"

"We can be friends, Ice, but I want more than that and you don't. I've lined up some dates with guys who don't think *marriage* is a dirty word."

Ice nodded, his eyes darkened, and he shoved his hand across his face. "Anyone I know?"

"Maybe." Not that it was any of his business. He was leaving. What did he care? "Just think the opposite of you."

He didn't seem to like that response. "The contractor?"

"For one."

"He seems like a nice guy. A bit dull maybe."

"Well, there's a realtor I know, and he's asked me for a drink."

His lips were pressed together. He nodded, looking away.

"And Callee and Quint know some great guys."

"Yeah, I'm sure they do. Will these guys be meeting the boys, taking them to the park, playing catch with Logan? Talking sports cars with Luke?"

If she didn't know better, she'd think he sounded pissed. "I won't marry any guy who doesn't also love my boys like his own. That's one of my priorities."

"So you're not looking to fall in love, you're just looking to find a daddy for those boys?"

"What's wrong with that?"

"I wouldn't want a wife who married me only so I could be a father to her kids."

"Well, you don't want a wife so that isn't likely to happen to you."

# Chapter Fifteen

⁓

Ice stood on the deck of his Malibu home, his gaze riveted on the crashing waves, the rhythm matching the pounding of his heart. What was the matter with him? Why couldn't he feel whatever the hell it was that had Bobby grinning at him like a besotted idiot?

Bobby lifted his glass of icy eggnog and whiskey in a celebratory cheer. "I appreciate the ride to LAX, man."

"I got nothing better to do today."

"Do you realize this will be the first Thanksgiving in the past seven or so years that we won't be together? If you'd told me last summer that you'd be spending this day at your mother's and that I'd be flying to Kalispell to dine at Chopper Henderson's house, I would have called bullshit!"

"Me too." But thanks to that amazing day he'd spent

with Andrea and her sons, he'd returned home realizing he needed to make some serious changes. He'd found a therapist, faced his demons, and finally accepted that the only way he would ever be whole again was to try and reconcile with his parents, or at the very least, forgive them. He'd been terrified, but he'd done it.

"So how'd it go with your old man?"

Ice took a drink. "Turns out he's not the dickhead I thought he was."

"Yeah, I figured once you understood how many times he's tried to offer an olive branch that he actually did want a relationship with you."

"I was too busy pushing him away." He'd finally told Bobby the events leading up to his parents' split when he was seven. And even that had made him feel better. Less alone.

"You gonna tell me what went down with your dad?"

"I paid a surprise visit to his office at iMagnus Studios."

"Holy shit."

Ice nodded. "I expected his private office would reflect his ruthless personality, but that was only one of the things I'd miscalculated. Everywhere I looked were framed news clippings and articles about me, large and small accomplishments I've had over the years. A bookshelf behind his desk had scrapbooks with my name on them. Inside were photos and report cards from the time I started boarding school through graduation. It blew me away."

"If he missed you that much, why didn't he just come and get you? Take you home?"

"He thought he was doing the right thing leaving me

there, protecting me. He'd been ill-advised by a school counselor, who told both of my parents that I needed stability, that the school environment could offer that better than two feuding parents using me in a game of tug-of-war."

"I hope they fired the bitch."

"Wouldn't know." Ice closed his eyes, recalling the meeting with his father. His dad, an older version of himself, had tears standing in his blue eyes, and his words rang fresh in Ice's mind. *"I'll understand, Ian, if you can't forgive me. I've never forgiven myself for the horrific thing I said to you on your seventh birthday."*

"I take it things worked out?"

"He wants me to spend Christmas with him in Aspen."

"Are you gonna?"

Ice smiled. "I'm thinking about it." He'd made Ice a business proposition he was also considering, but that was something he and Bobby could discuss once Ice had made up his mind.

"Wow, then I'd say you've got a lot to be thankful for this year, my friend. A whole lot."

"So do you. How's BiBi?"

Bobby's grin filled his eyes. "We're taking it slow, man. She's got some great ideas for a couple of reality shows. We're going to script them out while I'm there. You and I can discuss them next month."

"Meanwhile, we'd better get you to the airport."

\* \* \*

As Ice drove toward his mother's in Beverly Hills, toward the first Thanksgiving dinner with his family in twenty-some years, his mind traveled with Bobby to Kalispell. Standing in Andrea's little kitchen listening to her talk about moving on, he'd realized he couldn't move at all. Not forward or backward or even sideways. Holding on to the anger and hurt was destroying him, limiting his life to a series of hookups and letdowns. If that was all he faced ahead, he might as well walk into the Pacific.

His mother's pleading face filled his mind. "Can you, Ian? Can you forgive us?" She was all but strangling a lace handkerchief, her voice shaky. The power to hurt his parents, as they'd hurt him, was in his hands at that moment. All the things he'd wanted to say to them, the anger, the rage, the bone-deep pain of a scared, lonely, unloved little boy burst from the secret place into the light, but like vampires exposed to sunshine, the emotions shriveled and died, no longer monsters but a pile of cold, dead ashes. No longer able to hurt him. And he knew he did forgive them.

But somehow, he still felt dwarfed emotionally. Maybe it would take time. Or maybe he was so damaged he could never completely heal. Maybe he was destined to always be alone. To never find someone as wonderful as Andrea. He hoped she, however, could find the right guy.

He dialed Bobby, hoping to catch him before he boarded his plane. "I, er, if you see Andrea, or hear anything about her…"

"Why don't you call her yourself, man?"

"Naw, I didn't leave things exactly…you know?"

"But things have changed since then."

"Some things. Not everything. I'm still not—"

"You know what, man, you've forgiven everyone else, maybe you should forgive yourself."

"What the hell does that mean? I don't have anything to forgive myself for. I was seven years old. I didn't know a picture I took would destroy my family."

"That's right. You didn't. But you blame yourself all the same."

"No I don't." He started to tell Bobby to go screw himself, but the words stuck in his craw. As a memory surfaced, Ice nearly drove into oncoming traffic. He heard his seven-year-old self sobbing into his pillow every night, *"I'm sorry. I didn't mean to do it. It's my fault."* A light flared through his mind, a flame chasing off the darkness, burning away the shadows, exposing the truth. *Dear God, he did blame himself.* The realization left him reeling. "But it wasn't my bad."

"Exactly. I gotta go. Plane's boarding. Have a great Thanksgiving, man."

As Ice drove through the gates to his mother's mansion, he realized the frozen rock in the very center of his being was melting, dissolved by the blazing heat of self-forgiveness. He felt certain that if he looked in the rearview mirror, he wouldn't see Ice Erikksen, but the seven-year-old boy he'd been when he left this place. Ian Craig Whittendale had finally come home.

# Chapter Sixteen

Andrea was meeting Wade at Big Sky Pie to go over the plans for Emily's thirteenth birthday bash, and later they were taking her boys and his daughter to a new holiday family film the kids were anxious to see. He and Emily had spent Thanksgiving with her family at her mother's house, and it had been one of the best they'd celebrated in years.

She wasn't dating Wade exclusively, but he was easy to talk with, comfortable, fun, and definitely the kind of guy a woman could find a happily ever after with. But she wasn't anywhere close to that yet.

As she entered the pie shop through the back door and breathed in the delightful aromas of pumpkin, nutmeg, cinnamon, and apple, she had to smile. Did anything say "holidays" like that combination? Not in her opinion.

Jane and BiBi were in the process of finishing up for the day. Sales had been through the roof the past month, but would taper off over the next week and then gear up again before and during the Christmas season. Andrea greeted her coworkers, stowed her coat and purse, then went for a cup of coffee and readied the café to open. When she returned to the kitchen, they wanted to know how her Thanksgiving was and hear all the latest details of her romance with Wade.

She stood to one side, watching them work, as she started to tell them something cute the kids had done.

"That is some nice freezer," said a man, strolling in from the hallway to the cold room.

"Bobby?" Andrea's heart stuttered. What was he doing here? *Had Ice come with him?*

"Hey, Andrea," he said. "I was just admiring the new freezer."

"It was a gift from an anonymous donor," Jane said. Her pregnant belly had grown very large in the past few weeks. "Molly suspects Charlie Mercer's conscience got the better of him, but he adamantly denies that he bought it."

And Andrea believed him. He'd found a hole in the Freon line. It had definitely been sabotaged, and Charlie had had neither opportunity nor motive. Her money was on the TV crew as the culprits. "I'm sure that it was Ice's way of making up for the chaos and loss of revenue he caused the day the Health Department shut us down."

"Nope," Bobby said. "Ice didn't buy that freezer. Not through the business or personally. He'd have told me."

"How is Ice?" Andrea asked, trying to sound off-hand, hoping the whole room couldn't hear the thud-ding of her heart or the tremor in her voice. See her hands shake.

"He's better than ever. Really good. He spent Thanksgiving with his mother and is doing Christmas with his dad. He's started dating a gorgeous starlet. It's all good. Oh, I almost forgot, he said to tell you 'hi.' "

Spending the holidays with his parents? Something had definitely changed for Ice, and it sounded as though it was something good. But dating a starlet? She wanted to be happy that Ice was returning to the life he should always have had. So why wasn't she? Didn't she want him to heal? To move on? Of course she did.

*He'll be free to fall in love and marry someone in his social realm, a kingdom far removed from mine.*

"Then I wonder who did buy that freezer," Jane said, crimping the edge of a caramel apple pie crust. "The appliance store claims the person who'd purchased it lives somewhere in Flathead County."

Who else had something to gain by the freezer drama? Andrea wondered. But as she caught a know-ing exchange between BiBi and Bobby, it struck her that there was one other person with deep pockets and motive. Chopper Henderson. He'd wanted BiBi to have more air time, and he'd wanted his investment in the pilot to pay off when the show was picked up. She sus-pected BiBi knew it, too.

Andrea asked, "How long are you in town, Bobby?"

"That depends on BiBi."

BiBi took a big breath and offered up the wide grin of someone with news to share. "I told Molly and Quint yesterday, so it's not really a secret anymore. I'm moving to L.A. to work with Bobby."

Andrea's mouth dropped open. She knew BiBi and Bobby had stayed in touch, but she hadn't expected their relationship to escalate this quickly. She remembered Ice's words of caution. *Bobby is in the rebound phase.* An odd, older sister feeling swept through her, making her wonder if she should intervene or offer some been-there, done-that advice.

"What?" Jane sprinkled her sugary mix across the pies' top crusts, frowning at BiBi. "Bobby's hiring you as an assistant pastry chef?"

"No." BiBi laughed. "We're forming our own company, developing ideas for pilots. Daddy is going in as a silent partner, buying out Ice's share of the company."

"But what about Ice?" Jane asked. "What's he going to do then?"

Bobby scrubbed at his red beard. "He's had a better offer from his old man. He's joining the iMagnus Studios."

\* \* \*

Country music boomed off the walls of the reception hall, the live band playing a mix of popular rock and roll and classic romantic favorites. Dean and Betty Gardener had decided to put off the celebration of their marriage until two weeks after Thanksgiving. They'd changed their theme to red and green, and she was decked out in a red velvet, floor-length gown with a red and green plaid bow in her hair that matched Dean's vest and bow tie.

They were thrilled to have Big Sky Pie provide pies that ranged from key lime, to crème de menthe to frozen cherry. A prime rib buffet with champagne, beer, and cranberry punch with green ice cubes rounded out the menu.

Andrea, Logan, Lucas, and Delores had come with Wade and Emily and were seated at a round table enjoying the food. Molly had shown up with Charlie Mercer and kept reminding everyone that they were only friends, although it was obvious Charlie hoped for much more. Callee and Quint laughed and chatted with others, but never strayed far from each other, exchanging loving glances, even from across the room. She stopped by the table and whispered to Andrea that Roxy was moving back to Kalispell. She was going to buy a house and open a bistro in town. Callee was thrilled, and Andrea shared her delight. Roxy was a little wild and a whole lot of fun.

Nick Taziano passed by their table as he carried a plate of food to Jane. He'd never seemed happier, his dark eyes sparkling with joy whenever he glanced at his pregnant wife. He settled her into a chair between his father and mother, brought her milk, and rubbed her sore feet. The gazes they shared wrenched at Andrea's heart, driving home what she longed to have and, she had to admit to herself, she still hadn't found.

A slow tune began to play, and couples rushed onto

the dance floor. Wade held his hand out for her, and Andrea took it. He was a good, if not exciting, dancer, but she felt safe in his arms, like being held by a protective older brother, just not how a lover should feel.

"This was Sarah's and my song," Wade whispered in her ear, hardly the thing a woman wanted to hear from a man she was dating. "She really enjoyed wedding celebrations."

"You loved her a lot, didn't you?"

The melancholy on his handsome face nearly broke her heart. "I did. I guess I still do."

"Yeah." Andrea realized it was a good thing she wasn't falling in love with Wade. She wouldn't have stood a chance against Sarah's ghost. He was as unavailable now as he had been during his marriage and since her loss. "I don't think you're ready to let her go yet, Wade."

He frowned, then the tension lifted from him as though he'd been carrying a heavy burden. "I really like you, Andrea. And the boys. I just, I guess, I'm not ready."

"I understand."

"If I can make an honest observation, I don't think you are either."

Andrea blanched. "How did you know?"

"What's that old fifties song? Something about it's in your kisses."

That wasn't quite the title, but point taken. She nodded.

Wade grew serious, his expression tender. "I think you're hung up on some guy. I don't know who, but if I had to guess, I'd say it was that Ice Erikksen."

She wanted to deny it, but her tongue refused to form the words. "He doesn't want me either."

"Then he's a damned fool. And you're better off without him."

Mentally, she knew Wade was right. Emotionally, her heart refused to listen. She hadn't stopped wanting Ice. But he'd walked away and never looked back. Not one phone call or text. Just a message sent through Bobby.

She needed to face it. She couldn't compete with a starlet. Ice wasn't going to walk into this reception and sweep her off her feet. And he didn't.

\* \* \*

A week later, Andrea was interviewing potential assistant pastry chefs when who should walk into Big Sky Pie, but Rafael Sanchez. Rafe, a tall, handsome Latino, was the assistant chef who'd run off the day Molly had her heart attack. He'd thought he'd caused her collapse, that he'd killed her. Rafe spoke very little English and had gone into hiding, fearing he'd be sent to jail or back to Mexico.

Andrea had tried to find him and explain, to make sure his fear of being deported wasn't because he was in the United States illegally. She'd had no luck finding him, but did learn that he had a green card.

She led him into the kitchen. "Molly, look who's shown up."

"Oh, Rafe, I am so glad to see you."

Rafe said something in Spanish that sounded like he was even gladder to see Molly.

Andrea said, "He's here about the assistant pastry chef position. What do you think?"

Molly pinned Rafe with her bright eyes. "If I give you a second chance, you won't run off on me again, will you?"

"*No, señora.*"

"And you'll give us your actual phone number and address?" Andrea added.

"*Sí, señora.*"

Molly considered, then nodded. "The job's yours, Rafe. When can you start?"

"Now be good, *señora?*"

"*Sí,*" Molly said.

Andrea went back to the café. She had other interviewees scheduled, and although the assistant job had been filled, they would soon need a temporary chef while Jane was on maternity leave. At the end of the day, she was worn out. She wanted nothing more than to order a pizza and take a hot bath and hug her little sons. Her mom texted that she'd meet her at the apartment with the boys. Andrea had just walked into Moose's to order the pizza when her phone rang. It was Molly.

"Andrea dear, I hate to ask this, but I've just had a call from someone wanting to book an event. He's coming in right at closing. Could you possibly come back and handle this? If not, I'll find Callee to—"

"No, that's okay. I'm right across the street."

"Great. Thank you, dear."

Her worries this past autumn about the pie shop's future seemed a hundred years ago. Business was booming. This booking would be the last they could squeeze in before the New Year. Nothing like job security to boost a girl's spirits. So why were her Durangos dragging as she let herself in the back door of Big Sky Pie?

She knew why. She'd done something today she wasn't proud of. She'd gone online to the website that Rita Grace wrote for and hunted for tidbits about Ice. She'd found what she'd been after. He *was* dating a starlet—a gorgeous brunette who was starring in iMagnus's next action picture. She'd closed the browser, fighting tears, knowing that, once again, she'd fallen in love with a man who was wrong for her in every way. When would she ever learn?

The bell over the café door announced the arrival of the customer she'd been expecting. She checked her appearance in the mirror, applied some lip gloss, and hurried to greet him. Her bad-boy antenna began to buzz. He was seated in the shadows near the bay windows.

She braced herself and collected a menu. "Welcome to Big Sky Pie. May I get you something to drink?"

"Depends," he said in a drawl that rivaled Sam Elliott's gravelly voice and turned her knees to mush. Ice. He wore a white dress shirt beneath a leather jacket, torn jeans, and his Harley boots, as casual as a *GQ* ad, as sexy as a man could get. Her heart began to thud. He lifted his face, mirrored aviators hiding his eyes. "What are you offering?"

Tingles rocked through Andrea, and she almost responded, "My body," but then she remembered the brunette starlet and the words dissolved on her tongue. "We have milk, coffee, espresso, tea, and water."

"Espresso." He rattled off his favorite concoction.

"Venti, I suppose?"

"Sure."

Andrea laughed. "This isn't Starbucks. Our espresso is the basic brew."

"Then basic it is." Although the lighting was dim, she couldn't look away from his handsome face, his sexy mouth, couldn't help noticing that a new air of confidence had replaced his cockiness. This was not the wounded warrior she'd last seen.

He pulled off the aviators, exposing those intense blue eyes, and as his gaze swept over her, she swallowed hard. Memories slammed into her: Ice naked, Ice making love to her, Ice whispering sweet nothings. Her stomach dipped. *He's in love with someone else.* She turned to get his drink, but he stopped her. "Andrea?"

"Yes?" She didn't look at him. She couldn't. She stared at the espresso machine, its red light a familiar touchstone, something to keep her from sliding off the edge into unknown territory.

"What is that delightful scent?" Ice asked.

Her heart began to stumble in her chest. "It's the special of the—"

"I didn't come all this way for a piece of pie."

"Or to book an event?" *Like your wedding to the starlet?*

"Not that either."

She turned then, fighting the anger at being dragged

back to work on false pretenses, even if it was for this man she loved and longed to see again. "What are you doing here, Ice?"

He seemed to lose a touch of his confidence, as though he wasn't sure how to tell her. *He wants to tell me he's getting married.* Oh God, no. She didn't want to hear it. It would be less cruel to read about it on the Internet than to have him say those words to her.

He cleared his throat. "I came to claim something that's mine, unless I'm too late."

What did that mean? She was afraid to ask. Afraid the answer would be something she didn't want to hear. She poured a cup of espresso and brought it to his table. He reached for her wrist. She pulled away before he could grab it, went to the refrigerated display case, and placed a slice of pie on a dish, even though he'd said he wasn't here for pie. She kept chattering about the weather, about Jane and the baby coming soon, about Lucas getting his cast removed, about nothing. She served a scoop of ice cream atop the pie and brought it to him.

"Stop it. Please." Ice stood and caught her this time. "Just hear me out, and then, if you want me to go, I will."

"Start talking and make it quick. I need to get home to the boys."

He nodded. "Just tell me first if you've found a stepdaddy candidate yet."

She considered lying, but he'd see right through it. "Not yet."

That brought on his damnable, irresistible smile. "When I left you that last night, I hadn't thought I'd ever see you again. I couldn't offer you what you wanted, and I hated myself for that. Once I was back in Malibu, I realized that I had changed. Only the change was paralyzing. I was more emotionally stymied than before I came here. I'd touched on the possibility of something wonderful, but I didn't deserve it, and I couldn't hold on to it. Or claim it then."

"But now you can?" She clasped her hands together to keep them from trembling.

"A lot of things have changed for me."

"I know. Bobby says you've reconciled with your parents. That alone is huge—considering what they did to you."

"It was. But I couldn't move forward without forgiving them, and in the end, even that wasn't enough. I had to forgive myself."

"For what? You were a little boy..." Tears for what he'd been through sprang to her eyes and spilled down her cheeks. She swiped at them as he explained that he'd discovered he'd always blamed himself, and until he let go of that, he couldn't have a normal life.

She smiled at him through her tears, truly glad that he had found a way out of his personal darkness and into the light. "I'm glad for you, Ice. I really am. Bobby says you're working with your dad now."

"Well, sort of. I'm going to be doing something I discovered I'm pretty good at. Writing screenplays."

"You're giving up directing?"

"For the time being."

"Won't you miss that?"

"Not that much, I'm discovering. I guess it's all part of the moving on into the next phase of my life."

"Well, since you've been writing the scripts for the reality shows, I suppose writing screenplays won't be that far of a stretch for you."

He nodded. "And it's something I can do from anywhere. Even Kalispell. Actually, I've bought a place... in town."

In town? She gaped at him. "In this town?"

"Yeah, it's a huge, four-bedroom house with a great big backyard. Perfect for kids to run around, play football, race toy cars, have a dog."

If he was trying to stomp her heart into tiny pieces, he was doing a good job of it. Her voice cracked. "I guess we'll be seeing more of you then."

"Yes. I'm having the house gutted and remodeled. I've hired Wade to do the work, and Callee is going to work on the interior design. I'm hoping you'll help her with that."

"Me? Why would I?"

"I figured you'd like some say in how your new kitchen is laid out, the new fireplace, the bathrooms."

"My new kitchen?"

"I love you, Andrea. I want to marry you and be the father your sons need."

Had she heard him right? "What about the brunette starlet you've been squiring around Hollywood?"

"Publicity. She's my half sister on my mother's side. She inherited our mother's talent, but she wants to make it on her own merits, not by using the family name. Since I can relate to that sentiment, I have been giving her some pointers."

"Your sister? But Bobby said—"

"I'm sorry about that. The tabloids printed that lie, and I knew if I told Bobby the truth that he'd tell BiBi, and then she'd probably tell her father. So I didn't correct his misconception."

"In other words you turned the tables on the paparazzi?"

"I did. But I didn't mean for it to hurt you."

Andrea's heart was beating like a wild thing in her chest as she remembered the rest of what he'd said. He'd proposed. He had, hadn't he? She needed to hear it again. Needed to know it wasn't her imagination that he bought her a house and was moving to Kalispell. "Did you say you love me? You want to marry me?"

"My father once told me that life was like a pie, and I shouldn't settle for a slice when I could have the whole thing. I didn't understand what that meant until last week. I want the whole pie, Andrea. I want you, the boys, and any more that might come our way. But only if you feel the same about me."

Oh God, he *had* proposed. Andrea couldn't speak for fear that she was dreaming and she'd wake up if she said one word.

"You do love me, don't you? I can't stand it if I'm wrong about that."

"Oh, Ice, I love you so much it's killing me."

She leaped into his arms, he spun her around, and her feet crashed into the table. They jumped apart just as the dessert plate holding the pie à la mode skittered to the edge, then catapulted upward. The plate gained height, then gravity snatched at it, and it collided with Ice's pants before clattering to the floor.

He stood there with ice cream and pie dripping off the front of his jeans. He shook his head, laughing. "This is how we started."

Andrea wasn't letting anything come between them, not even Molly McCoy's pie. "But it's not how we'll finish. Hey, wait a minute. Who exactly am I agreeing to marry? Ice Erikksen or Ian Whittendale?"

"Ian Erikksen. Ice is too cold of a name for the man I am now. And since Erikksen is my legal name, it's less likely to require long explanations to the folks who already know me in my new hometown."

"Well, I love you no matter what your name is. But Lucas may still call you Ize."

Ian took her face in both his hands and peered at her with such love. "I hope, one day, he'll call me Dad."

Tears of joy spilled from Andrea's eyes.

"We better make this official," Ian said, pulling something from his pocket, and as he went down on one knee, Molly's words came rushing back to her. *A couple of bites of my caramel apple pie and a man will look puppy-eyed at you. A whole slice, and he's liable to get down on one knee and offer a ring.*

Apparently it worked, even if the man didn't actually eat the pie.

# Molly McCoy's Granny Smith Caramel Apple Pie

## Crust

- 2½ cups all-purpose flour, plus extra for rolling
- 1 teaspoon salt
- 1 teaspoon sugar, plus extra for final sprinkling
- 1 cup (2 sticks or 8 ounces) unsalted butter, very cold, cut into ½-inch cubes
- 6 to 8 tablespoons ice water
- 1 egg, lightly beaten with 1 tablespoon of water

## Filling

- 35 caramels
- 1 tablespoon water
- 6 or 7 Granny Smith apples, peeled, cored, and thinly sliced
- ¾ to 1 cup sugar
- 2 tablespoons flour
- ½ to 1 teaspoon cinnamon
- dash of nutmeg
- dash of salt
- 2 tablespoons unsalted butter to dot on the top

To make the crust: Combine the flour, salt, and sugar in a food processor. Pulse until mixed. Add the cubed butter. Pulse 6 or 8 times until the butter is pea-sized and the mixture looks like coarse meal. Next add the ice water 1 tablespoon at a time. Pulse until the mixture just begins to clump. If you pinch some of the crumbly dough and it holds together, it's ready. If the dough doesn't hold together, add a little more water and pulse again. Caution: Too much water will make the crust tough.

Place the dough in a mound on a clean surface. Shape the dough mixture into two disks, one for the bottom crust, one for the top. Work the dough gently to form the disks. Don't overknead. You should be able to see flecks of butter in the dough. They will result in a flakier crust. Sprinkle a little flour around the disks. Wrap each disk in plastic wrap and refrigerate from 1 hour to 2 days.

Remove a crust disk from the refrigerator. Let it sit at room temperature for 5 to 10 minutes. This will soften it enough for easier rolling. On a lightly floured surface, roll out the dough to a 12-inch circle about 1/8-inch thick. If the dough begins to stick to the surface below, sprinkle some flour underneath. Carefully place the bottom crust into a 9-inch pie pan, pressing the dough gently into the bottom and sides of the pan. Trim the excess dough, leaving about 1/2 inch more than the edge of the pan.

To make the filling: Melt the caramels and water in a double boiler or metal bowl over simmering water;

heat for 10 minutes or until the caramels are partially melted. Cover and set aside, keeping the caramels in the pan over the heated water.

Peel and core the apples, then slice thinly so that they will be soft when cooked. Combine the sugar, flour, spices, and salt. Mix with the apples. Add the melted caramels and stir to mix. Pour into the pie shell. Dot butter across the filling.

Remove the other crust disk from the refrigerator, let it sit at room temperature for 5 to 10 minutes, then roll it into a 12-inch circle about 1/8-inch thick. Add the top crust to the pie, then crimp and flute the edges. Lightly brush the top crust with an egg wash made by whisking 1 large egg with 1 tablespoon of water, sprinkle sugar on top for sparkle, and then score the top crust with 4 slices.

Preheat the oven to 400°. Place the pie on the middle rack with a cookie sheet beneath to catch any filling that bubbles over. Bake for 50 minutes.

Let the pie cool before serving. Serve cold, or warm the pie and serve with ice cream.

Hunky, straightlaced contractor
Wade Reynolds has been hired
to remodel the storefront next to
Big Sky Pie. But when a red-hot
bad girl sets up shop there, she
may just be the decadent thing
he needs...

Please see the next page
for a preview of

*Decadent*

# Chapter One

*Going home under these circumstances was like over-indulging in decadent chocolate pie; the tummy ache outweighed the pleasure.*

"There he is." Roxanne Nash directed the driver of the hired car to pull over in the parking garage. "I'll just be a minute."

"Make sure, lady, 'cause I don't want that cat decidin' my ride is a giant litter box."

"She won't." But would she? Roxy bit her lower lip and glanced toward the cat carrier at her feet. Tallulah, her adopted, purebred Ragdoll had a mind of her own. Another reason to quickly scratch this last item off her get-out-of-Seattle-forever list.

Chill air slipped through her thin jacket as she exited the dark sedan and glanced around. She half-expected some of the reporters who'd assailed her at the hotel a while ago to be lurking behind parked cars, seeking one last sound bite in the final chapter of celebrity chef Roxanne Nash and Seahawks linebacker Ty Buckholtz. But there was only herself, her driver, and the man in the five-thousand-dollar suit.

She strode toward him, her high-heel boots clicking on the concrete floor, echoing through the vast space that was already filled to capacity with cars on this early Friday morning. The man, her ex's attorney, was standing next to a brown Escalade with a grille the same gleaming silver as her favorite sauté pan. She'd expected to meet him in his office on the 29th floor and was surprised that he'd suggested this instead. Although it would expedite their transaction. And given Tallulah's unpredictable nature, that was a good thing.

Roxy was here to pick up her half of the divorce settlement. So why was the attorney holding a set of keys and a file folder instead of a check-sized envelope? More curious yet, the attorney's normally unflappable manner showed signs of deteriorating. His tie was askew, his pocket square rumpled, and despite the cold, sweat beaded on his forehead. But most worrisome was his expression. It belonged on a surgeon about to deliver the news that his patient had died on the operating table.

A shiver that had nothing to do with the weather snaked down her spine. Something was amiss. But what? Myriad candidates leapt to mind, too many to pinpoint just one. *Stop it, Roxy. Whatever it is, it's not your problem. Just like Ty is no longer your problem.*

Buoyed by that thought, she stopped before the attorney, a paunchy, middle-aged man several inches shorter than her five-eleven. He'd applied his cologne with a heavy hand. The sharp odor mixed with the oily gasoline fumes and produced a nauseating stench. She stifled the urge to cover her nose as she ground to a halt. She didn't bother with niceties. Too much water had passed beneath the bridge between this lawyer and herself to pretend otherwise. Roxy held out her hand. "My check?"

The attorney shuffled from foot to foot, glanced away, then back at her like a shifty salesman about to offer her a bogus deal. Roxy wished her attorney were here, taking care of this, but that one-woman legal firm had decided to elope and take an extended honeymoon. *Probably on the money she'd earned representing me.*

The man cleared his throat. "Mr. Buckholtz has been trying to reach you since yesterday afternoon, Ms. Nash."

"Well, here's the thing about that," Roxy said, tilting her head to one side and smiling wide. "I no longer have to take his calls."

And she wouldn't. She'd blocked Ty's number on her cell phone.

"Or mine?"

Her silence seemed to grate on him.

"Well, Ms. Nash, if you'd answered our calls, it would have made this easier."

"Nothing could be easier than you giving me the money that I'm owed and me getting back in that car and catching the plane to Montana." She held her hand out again.

"I'm afraid I don't have the check."

He did not just say that. Exasperation twisted through her. "Why not?"

"There's been a . . . a complication."

She shivered, feeling the chill reach her bones. She should have opted for something warmer this morning, instead of choosing this lightweight jacket that matched her sage eyes and perfectly set off her layered mop of red hair, the style and shape likely slipping away in this damp air. But then, she hadn't planned on being outside this long. "What's the problem? Cut to the chase."

He pursed his lips, obviously more used to giving orders than taking them. "The sale of your house didn't close yesterday."

Of all the things she'd imagined being wrong, this had been low on the list. A knot began forming in her stomach. Ty had signed the closing papers yesterday morning. She'd signed an hour later, and the buyers were supposed to sign right after her. "What happened?"

"The buyers didn't show up at the title company."

"They backed out?" At the last freakin' minute? She tried calculating how much this would affect the plans she'd been making for her future in Kalispell, but she couldn't even assimilate the news.

"Well, no. They haven't exactly backed out. They just need an extension."

"On the closing?" They'd already been given two extensions.

"Yes." He looked as relieved as if he'd finally presented the problem in such simple terms a whole courtroom would understand, not realizing he'd omitted the important details. If he was a chef in her kitchen, she'd reprimand him for leaving out essential ingredients.

"The Dillons are already living in the house," she said, irritation clipping her words. Damn it. She'd trusted that couple enough to let them move into the house before the sale closed. Ty and her attorney had advised against this, but Roxy believed the Dillons sincerely meant to go through with the deal. *Obviously trusting the wrong people is a flaw I need to work on.* She didn't like being made a fool of. "They need to close as scheduled or get out so we can sell the house to someone else."

"Mrs. Dillon had a heart attack on the way to the title company's office."

Roxy froze, her ire squelched by contrition and concern. "Oh my God, d—did she die?"

"No, but apparently the situation was dire. Narrowed artery. Blood clot. She's having a stent inserted this morning, and she should be as good as new in a few days."

Relief flooded through Roxy. "Do you have the paperwork for the extension?" He gave it to her, and she signed it. Then she added, "You can FedEx me the check once the sale is finalized. And now, I'll take the check Ty is giving me for the bistro. I assume you have that."

The hired car's motor revved. Roxy glanced at the driver. He was scowling, pointing to his watch.

She nodded, then peered expectantly at the attorney. "As you can see, I need to get going."

The lawyer looked peaked, as if he might be ill.

"What?"

"Have you been hiding in a cave the past twenty-eight hours?"

What she'd been doing was none of his business. "I don't understand."

"Haven't you seen a news report or watched TV since yesterday?"

Her TV was on its way to Kalispell. And she had no interest in watching the news. It was bad enough dealing with the paparazzi outside the hotel this morning, shouting questions about Ty. Humming loudly inside her head, she'd simply tuned them out. "I've had all the media I can take for a while, thank you very much."

The driver of her hired car raced the engine, another prodding reminder that he wanted the cat out of the car and that the plane wasn't going to wait for her. She gave the driver an "I'm moving as fast as I can" glare, then told the attorney, "Look, I have to go right now. Please give me the bistro check."

"I can't."

"Why not?" What kind of trick was Ty pulling now?

"It's easier to just show you." The attorney produced an iPhone and pulled up an ESPN website. Finding what he wanted, he held the screen toward her.

Roxy protested, "I don't have time for this..."

Ty's name was a banner across the top of the national

sports report. The sportscaster said, "Seattle Seahawk Ty Buckholtz is being benched for the next four games due to alleged substance abuse issues."

Roxy just shook her head.

"Don't worry, Ms. Nash. We're appealing."

"I'm not worried." Roxy blew out an angry breath. She wasn't surprised that someone with Ty's low moral compass might be doing drugs. But it had nothing to do with her. She said, "Not my problem."

"Well, it sort of is." The attorney gnashed his teeth. "You see, Mr. Buckholtz has no access to his financial accounts and can't come up with the hundred thousand in cash that he promised you for turning over the bistro to him. His salary is frozen, and will be until he's cleared to play again. But he isn't trying to get out of his obligation to you. He's giving you something of equal value for collateral."

Collateral? "I'm not a bank or a pawn shop. I don't want anything but that cash."

"I've already explained that cash is not an option at this time."

She frowned, her foot tapping like a butcher knife through a pile of onions.

The hired car's engine revved again. She waved at the driver, praying Tallulah was behaving and would continue to do so for a few more minutes. She glared at the lawyer. "What is Ty offering me?"

The attorney held up the set of keys and pointed to the SUV with the gleaming-grille. "This Escalade."

Her gaze went to the four-door, truck-bed Cadillac

that shone like a gigantic chocolate diamond, the color more mocha than brown.

"It's a 2014 with every whistle and bell imaginable and more. It's worth as much as he owes you."

"Tell your client to send it back to the dealer and pay me the cash he owes me."

"He special ordered it. There's nothing wrong with it. He just can't return it. It's only until his salary is reinstated. Once that happens, Mr. Buckholtz will cut you a check and reclaim this vehicle. I have the legal documentation here. Already signed by my client."

"But I don't want it." She felt her plans slipping away like steam being sucked up a hood vent.

"I'm sorry, Ms. Nash." The lawyer shrugged. "It's this or nothing."

The dark sedan's engine revved once more. Roxy's nerves pinched. If she didn't leave this minute, the plane would be gone. She had to cut bait. Now. "How am I supposed to get the Cadillac to Montana?"

"I'll arrange to have it shipped." The attorney rattled off his intention of ordering a closed trailer to avoid road damage as he pocketed the keys.

Her mind was whirring faster than the blades of a blender. "I'd have to have the title in my name."

"That's already been done." He handed her the paper-work. She inspected the documentation, reading fast, glad to find there were no hidden clauses. She signed it.

"And you'll arrange shipping today?" she asked, returning his pen.

"As soon as I get to my office."

Could she take him at his word? Probably. He wouldn't stay in business long if he pulled something as unethical as not following through on a signed contract. But add Ty into the mix and all bets were off. What if she walked out of this garage with only the title and a signed agreement, and the vehicle somehow didn't get sent? What if she had to go back to court to get her hundred thousand dollars? She shuddered at how much that might end up costing. Her attorney would probably retire on it. She decided that—despite the eleven- to twelve-hour drive-time involved—the simplest solution was the best. "Or I could drive it to Montana."

The lawyer's brows lifted. "You could, but I must caution you to be extremely careful. The Escalade needs to come back to Mr. Buckholtz in exactly the same condition as it leaves here."

"Yeah, well, tell him to worry about himself. The Cadillac is under full warranty, and I'm holding the proof of insurance. So potential mishaps are covered." *Romance should come with collision and liability insurance,* Roxy thought. *That way when a woman collides with a potential love interest, she'll be covered when he becomes a liability.*

* * *

Wade Reynolds' Friday night was off to a bad start. He felt like he'd stepped on a bear trap, caught by inescapable jaws, the pain so fierce he couldn't release the screaming in his brain. He glanced at his twelve-year-old daughter for help, but the hopeful gleam in her eyes sent an arrow through his heart. *Et tu, Emily?* Damn. His beloved little girl was in on this, this…female setup. Why did everyone seem intent on hooking him up? Was he wearing a sign around his neck: Widower seeking mate? Hell no. Just the opposite. His wedding band should deter any such ill-advised action. So what if it had been four years since cancer took Sarah? He still didn't want anyone else. Not now. Not ever.

He stammered, "I, uh, I, uh, can't stay for dinner."

The sexily clad single mother of Emily's best friend dropped her smile like he would drop an overheated nail gun. "But the table's set and—"

"I have plans." It was the truth, but Wade felt his neck getting warm as he threaded the brim of his Stetson through nervous fingers, and he knew it looked like he was pulling excuses from his hat. He backed toward the door. "I'm sorry, but if I don't leave now, I'll be late."

The pretty blonde rushed toward him, her boobs bouncing in the V-neck of her sweater like bobbers on a lake, teasing that a strike was imminent. The thought sent a flash of fear through him. He said, "Emily, I'll pick you up tomorrow around noon."

"Awww, Dad." The look of disappointment in his daughter's eyes fueled his distress.

"I can bring her home," said the blonde—Tiffany or Taffy or Tippy—sashaying closer still, every switch of her hips suggestive, seductive.

Wade's blood began to heat, his body reacting to the stimuli. Hell, he was human. And hetero. And deprived.

He saw a cold shower in his near future. "Sure. Okay. I'll call Emily tomorrow."

With that, Wade slipped on his hat and hastened out the door, making sure to shut it behind him. He stood on the porch, breathing hard, the cold air flushing relief through his overheated body. Biting wind swirled snow across the front walk and into his face. He'd only been inside ten minutes and already another three inches of the white stuff had piled onto the yard and street, big sloppy flakes, the kind that stick so fast they turn roads into ice rinks. He pulled up the collar of his sheepskin jacket and trudged to his pickup, arriving at the driver's side feeling like a snowman.

He kicked the compacted flakes from his boots, brushed off his hat and shoulders, the effort futile, the snow piling back on faster than he could smack it away. He climbed into the cab and got the engine running. The wipers *swicked* across the windshield, clearing a small quadrant of visibility. Still fuming mad, he clamped his hands on the steering wheel as he jammed his foot on the gas pedal. The pickup lurched, the tires skidding, the truck bed barely missing a mailbox. He eased off the gas, but anger continued to boil through him, anger at being set up, anger at himself for being unable to get past Sarah's death, to let go of the guilt. How could Emily have had any part in this? Yeah, she was a kid, but still…It seemed so disloyal to her mother.

This had Callee McCoy's handiwork written all over it. He thought back to earlier in the week. Callee, the wife of his best friend, was working as a design consultant on a remodel job he was doing. She'd come to his house to discuss a change to the kitchen they were overhauling. Emily had wandered in while he'd stepped out to take a phone call, and when he'd returned, the two females had their heads together, discussing something like crooks plotting a crime.

He hadn't known then that he'd been the intended victim.

He considered calling Quint, Callee's husband, and canceling his plans to meet them at the pie shop before heading over to Moose's Saloon for pizza and beer. But Quint would ask why, and Wade doubted he'd get any sympathy once he told him. Quint was president of the Get Wade Laid Club.

Wade tossed his hat onto the passenger seat. His friends meant well, but he wished they'd listen to him and just stop. Maybe he should skip the pizza and beer and grab a burger to eat at home. Alone. In that big empty house. Maybe a movie then. Alone. The thought made him queasy. Lately he'd been feeling it more and more, a deep loneliness settling over him that was thicker than the snow on his hood.

If he was honest with himself, he'd admit he missed having a woman in his life. Just saying it in his head seemed to unlock a floodgate and fill him with a yearning he'd denied for too long. Damn, how he missed female companionship, missed the interaction of conversation, missed the warmth a woman brought to a home. Missed the closeness. The sex. Especially the sex.

He twisted the gold band on his left ring finger. He'd tried dating a few weeks back, but had to end it when he realized he wasn't going to move the relationship beyond friendship. He didn't want a romance, didn't want to fall in love. Although he wouldn't mind someone to go to the movies with, and maybe a little more, occasionally—someone who didn't expect or want anything permanent from him. An image of the perfect candidate filled his mind: a tiny blonde, as demure and even-tempered as his Sarah had been.

* * *

Roxy squinted against the snow pinging like pellets against the windshield. The road was a solid sheet of white. Only the tracks made by other drivers assured her that she wasn't headed for a ditch, but the tread marks were quickly disappearing beneath a fresh layer of white. She yawned and rubbed at her weary eyes. Twelve hours on the road. If she'd known it would be snowing, she'd have stopped in Spokane and made the rest of the trip tomorrow, in daylight. One of the gadgets on the dashboard probably included a weather app, if she could figure out how to operate it, but there had been no time to study a manual. And besides, she'd been lulled into a false confidence by the ease of driving this luxurious, 4-wheel drive Escalade until it was too late to turn back.

She shifted in the seat, trying to relieve the numbness in her bottom and to get the blood moving in her legs. She longed for a place to get out and stretch, but then Tallulah would also want out, and just imagining the cat's reaction to all the white stuff made Roxy shudder. No telling how the cat would react to snow. Fortunately, another mile should see them pulling up to her mother's house in Kalispell.

A sudden glare of light pierced her thoughts. Roxy jolted. Headlights roared toward the passenger side of the Escalade. Holy shit. A giant pickup truck was about to T-bone the Cadillac. She slammed the brakes. Her vehicle fishtailed, then started to pirouette like an ice skater. The scream she reserved for riding roller coasters filled the cab as she held the steering wheel in a death grip and slammed her eyes shut, bracing for the collision.

With every muscle clenched, she didn't realize for several seconds that the Escalade had stopped spinning. Or that she'd felt no impact. Nothing. Not a bump. Or a crunch. No air bags exploding. Just a sudden silence punctuated by the roar of her pulse. She opened her eyes. The Escalade was now pointed nose to nose with the pickup as if they were about to kiss. Her heart tried to escape through her throat. Her breath came in rapid punches.

Curse words spewed from her mouth as she stumbled out of her vehicle to confront the jerk driving the pickup, a mountainous man in a light-colored Stetson and sheepskin jacket. He emerged through the heavy snowfall like the Marlboro Man coming to rescue the damsel in distress. It had been a long, disappointing, frustrating day, and Roxy's temper was as shredded as a pile of cheddar. She didn't need rescuing. Especially not by some idiot who didn't know how to drive in snow. "What the hell were you thinking, you jackass? Speeding in these conditions? Are you nuts?"

He stopped in his tracks, caught between the front fenders of the vehicles, the headlights exposing a handsome, amused face with a slow, sexy grin. "I'm sorry, ma'am. I just wanted to make sure you weren't harmed."

"Only by the grace of God," she huffed. The huge, fat flakes seemed to have muted the world around them, giving her the sense that they were alone in the wilderness rather than on a normally busy highway.

She reined in her temper with a struggle. She wasn't hurt. The Escalade wasn't damaged. She needed to calm down, but that was easier said than done given the adrenaline still rushing through her. "You're right. I'm okay. No harm, no foul."

"Exactly . . . and if you hadn't hit your brakes—"

"If I hadn't—?" A new flare of ire spiked through her. *Welcome home, Roxy, to good old redneck country—where macho reigns supreme.* "You're the one who came roaring out of the side road at breakneck speed, buddy. Not me."

"I wasn't speeding." He shook his head, eyed her license plate, and then offered up that slow, sexy grin again. "Driving in snow takes a certain skill that most Seattleites aren't familiar with."

She recalled the Escalade had the name of the auto dealership on the license plate frame. She narrowed her eyes wanting to call him on making assumptions, on jumping to conclusions, but then she'd done the same, assuming he couldn't drive in this weather. Instead, she opted to undermine his macho swagger. "I'll have you know that I cut my driving teeth just down the street from here, during an ice storm."

But he was no longer listening, or looking at her. His attention had snagged on the Escalade like a gourmand eyeing his favorite dish. He released a low whistle of appreciation. "It would've been a shame to damage this baby. It looks almost new."

"Almost?" Roxy choked on the word. *Try new, hot-off-the-showroom-floor-that-morning.* Ty hadn't even driven it yet—which offered the only trace of satisfaction she'd felt since discovering she wasn't going to get the money owed her today. "It was a consolation prize."

"Really." He sounded surprised. "If this is the consolation, what did the winner get?"

*My life.* "What she deserves."

That caught his full attention. He looked up, shoving his Stetson back enough to give her a glimpse of his eyes, some pale, warm color. Roxy squared her shoulders expecting him to ask her to explain the remark, but instead he yanked off the hat, plowed his fingers through hair the same mocha color as the Cadillac, and offered her a sympathetic, "I see."

He couldn't possibly "see" what she'd been through, but his kindness and unassuming manner pulled her off balance. He'd circled the Escalade and was trudging toward her from the rear. He said, "Since no damage has been done to either of our vehicles, we should probably get out of the middle of this road. All manner of fools venture out in this weather."

She stiffened. Was that another dig at her? Or was she just too tired and too sensitive? She swallowed a new knot of pique. Tallulah and she—"Oh my God, Tallulah!"

She lunged for the back door of the Escalade and yanked it open, almost slamming it into Marlboro Man's gut. A yowl escaped into the chilly night.

"Is your child hurt?" He hovered over her, alarm in his deep voice.

"Tallulah isn't a child. She's a Ragdoll." The interior light shone on the cat carrier. Its door was ajar. She reached inside. Empty. Alarm shot through Roxy. She tried backing up, but Marlboro Man stood too close, blocking her retreat.

"A what?" He leaned over her shoulder, peering into the Cadillac. "Is that some sort of gerbil?"

"Back up. Quick." Her heel sank into the toe of his boot. He jerked just as a ball of fur flew past the right side of Roxy's face. The tall cowboy gasped, then swore. Roxy spun around, frantic to grab the cat. Tallulah clung to the collar of the man's sheepskin jacket like a rabid raccoon, hissing, while Marlboro Man grappled to remove her. Roxy reached for the big feline, tripped on the toe of his boot, and fell hard against him, knocking him backward. He dropped to the road, his Stetson flying off, landing just beyond his head, brim side up.

Tallulah leaped for the hat as Roxy landed on top of the man. Air woofed from his lungs. And hers. She scrambled to lift herself from him, frantic to catch the cat before it escaped into the wild, but she slipped on the compacted snow and ice, landing on him a second time, her nose ending up buried against his neck. Oh Lord, he smelled like a fresh summer breeze with a hint of something spicy, and felt so male that her body clenched.

She pushed up on his chest, and his gaze locked on hers. She felt his arousal against her thigh and felt her face glowing with the heat of humiliation, her flesh alive with lust. A charged awareness passed between them, startling her. It seemed to startle him, too. He released a guttural moan, catching hold of her, rolling sideways, and then disentangling his long legs from hers. "Where's that critter?"

As he helped her to her feet, Roxy spotted Tallulah balancing on the brim of the Stetson, and she realized that, in the pale light, it resembled the rim of a commode. The cat didn't use a litter box. She was toilet-trained. "Oh, no, Tallulah, don't!"

But the cat wasn't paying any attention to Roxy. She assumed the position and relieved herself into the bowl of the hat.

"Oh God." Roxy grimaced.

"What the—?" Horror etched Marlboro Man's face, but he waited until the cat was finished, then snatched the hefty feline by the scruff and gently handed her to Roxy. "This is yours, I believe."

"Oh God, I'm so sorry," she said, silently admonishing Tallulah as she placed her back in the cat carrier and secured the latch. "I'll pay to have it cleaned."

He snorted. "Cleaning won't fix this."

"You're right, of course. If you'll give me your name and number, I'll buy you a new one. Exactly like this one."

He shrugged, shook the snow from his thick hair, and flashed that slow, sexy smile again. "Don't worry about it. Shit happens. The hat wasn't new, and besides, I have others."

"Are you sure?" This wasn't right. She had to make it up to him.

"Positive." He lifted the fouled hat by the brim, emptied it, carried it to his pickup, and tossed it into the bed. As he made his way to the cab of his truck, his cell phone rang. She heard him answer it. "Wade Reynolds speaking."

Roxy settled onto her driver's seat, catching one last glimpse of the sexy cowboy named Wade Reynolds as she backed away from his vehicle and pointed the Escalade for town. A moment later, his headlights filled her rearview mirror. Following. A sensuous quiver swept through her as she recalled her reaction to his inviting smell, and his reaction to her laying on top of him. She hadn't been with a man since figuring out she couldn't forgive and forget Ty's betrayals; she was beyond ready for a love affair or two or even three. And considering the sparks that had just flown between them, she was putting Wade Reynolds at the top of her "to-do" list.

Unless he was married, engaged, or involved. She'd be damned if she'd poach another woman's man.

"Wade Reynolds...hmm. Why does that name sound so familiar, Tallulah?"

The cat wasn't paying any attention. She'd gone back to sleep. The little monster had no conscience. As Roxy reached the outskirts of town, she remembered where she'd heard Marlboro Man's name. He was one of Callee and Quint McCoy's best friends. In fact, Wade and Callee were working on a home renovation together.

He wasn't married, engaged, or in a relationship. He was a widower, still grieving the loss of his wife, despite four years having passed since her death and despite his friends trying to get him to move on. Roxy began to smile. What could be better? He had to be as primed for some hot monkey sex as she was, and he wouldn't want any kind of clingy, messy relationship since he was still in love with his deceased wife. That suited Roxy to a T. She was never, ever falling in love again. Never getting married again.

But what else had Callee said about Wade? Oh yeah. "He's laced up tighter than the sneakers he wore winning the state basketball championship his senior year of high school."

Roxy smiled. "What do you think, Tallulah? Wouldn't it be fun to unlace the sexy Mr. Reynolds?"

## *Fall in Love with Forever Romance*

### LAST CHANCE FAMILY
### by Hope Ramsay

Mike Taggart may be a high roller in Las Vegas, but is he ready to take a gamble on love in Last Chance? Fans of Debbie Macomber, Robyn Carr, and Sherryl Woods will love this sassy and heartwarming story from *USA Today* bestselling author Hope Ramsay.

### SUGAR'S TWICE AS SWEET
### by Marina Adair

Fans of Jill Shalvis, Rachel Gibson, and Carly Phillips will enjoy this sexy and sweet romance about a woman who's renovating her beloved grandmother's house—even though she doesn't know a nut from a bolt—and the bad boy who can't resist helping her... even as she steals his heart!

## *Fall in Love with Forever Romance*

### ALL FOR YOU
### by Jessica Scott

Fans of JoAnn Ross and Brenda Novak will love this poignant and emotional military romance about a battle-scarred warrior who fears combat is the only escape from the demons that haunt him, and the woman determined to show him that the power of love can overcome anything.

### DELIGHTFUL
### by Adrianne Lee

Pie shop manager Andrea Lovette always picks the bad boys, and no one is badder than TV producer Ice Erickksen. Andrea knows she needs to find a good family man, so why does this bad boy still seem like such a good idea? Fans of Robyn Carr and Sherryl Woods will eat this one up!

*Fall in Love with Forever Romance*

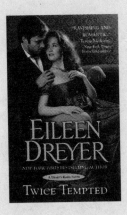

### TWICE TEMPTED
**by Eileen Dreyer**

As two sisters each discover love, *New York Times* bestselling author Eileen Dreyer delivers twice the fun in her newest of the Drake's Rakes Regency series, which will appeal to fans of Mary Balogh and Eloisa James.

### A BRIDE FOR
### THE SEASON
**by Jennifer Delamere**

Can a wallflower and a rake find happily ever after in each other's arms? Jennifer Delamere's Love's Grace trilogy comes to a stunning conclusion.